# What Could Go Wrong?

## WILLO DAVIS ROBERTS

**ALADDIN**

NEW YORK   LONDON   TORONTO   SYDNEY   NEW DELHI

ALADDIN

An imprint of Simon & Schuster Children's Publishing Division
1230 Avenue of the Americas, New York, New York 10020
This Aladdin hardcover edition September 2016
Text copyright © 1989 by Willo Davis Roberts
Jacket illustration copyright © 2016 by Jessica Handelman
Also available in an Aladdin paperback edition.
All rights reserved, including the right of reproduction
in whole or in part in any form.
ALADDIN is a trademark of Simon & Schuster, Inc., and related logo
is a registered trademark of Simon & Schuster, Inc.
For information about special discounts for bulk purchases,
please contact Simon & Schuster Special Sales at 1-866-506-1949
or business@simonandschuster.com.
The Simon & Schuster Speakers Bureau can bring authors
to your live event. For more information or to book an event contact
the Simon & Schuster Speakers Bureau at 1-866-248-3049
or visit our website at www.simonspeakers.com.
Jacket designed by Jessica Handelman
Interior designed by Mike Rosamilia
The text of this book was set in New Century Schoolbook.
Manufactured in the United States of America 0816 FFG
2 4 6 8 10 9 7 5 3 1
Library of Congress Control Number 2016945593
ISBN 978-1-4814-7490-0 (hc)
ISBN 978-1-4814-7489-4 (pbk)
ISBN 978-1-4814-7491-7 (eBook)

*For Joshua, whose adventure
inspired this story*

# Chapter one

Every other summer we have a family reunion. Aunts and uncles and cousins come from all over the country to spend a week together, having fun. Having fun means mostly eating a lot and sitting around talking, if you're a grown-up, or eating a lot and playing games and swimming if you're a kid.

There are plenty of kids. My mom has three brothers and two sisters, and except for Aunt Molly they all have kids. Some of my cousins are great—like Charlie—and some of them are jerks—like Cheryl. The rest are in between. I'm Gracie Cameron, and I'm eleven.

The Portwood side of the family all look alike, including my mom. They have dark hair and brown eyes. They talk a lot—too much, my dad says, and every year there's a reunion he wants to know why it can't be just for a weekend or over a three-day holiday instead of for a whole week. He says it's a good thing we only have the reunions every other year, because he couldn't stand that many Portwoods any oftener.

This last summer the reunion was held at Grandpa and Grandma Portwood's. This wasn't such a treat for my brother, Max, and me, because we live only six miles from them and we go there all the time. (Dad likes Portwoods okay in fewer numbers.) But it's a good place for a reunion, because they have a farm and there are so many things to do, like fish or swim in the Pilchuck River or milk cows. Unless you're like Cheryl; she wouldn't think of going in the barn or touching a cow.

Grandma and Grandpa Portwood also have a huge house, with five bedrooms and a big front porch where the kids could sleep in sleeping bags. That was fun, too, except that Uncle George and Aunt Monica slept in the front downstairs bedroom, with the window open, and Uncle George kept saying, "You kids stop giggling and go to sleep." Cheryl was the only one who shut up before Uncle George got up and closed the window.

Uncle Jim and Aunt Lila didn't sleep in the house. They parked their motor home on the front lawn—Grandpa's not very particular about his lawn, says he doesn't have time to keep it mowed, anyway—and Charlie has his own bunk in it, but he slept on the porch with the rest of us kids.

We were the last ones to get to the farm, even if we did live the closest. Dad kept finding things he had to do right up to the last minute until Mom said, "Donald Cameron, if you aren't in the car in five minutes, we're going without you."

Dad said, "Is that a promise?" She gave him one of her looks and he sighed and said, "Okay. Let me get something to take along to read."

Dad's the only one who reads at a reunion. He says he only does it after his ears ache from too much conversation.

We could see everyone else had already arrived. There were cars parked everywhere. Old Jack, Grandpa's collie, came out and barked a welcome, wagging his tail. Max hugged him and then ran toward the kitchen, hoping Grandma would have something to eat to last us until suppertime. She almost always did.

I was looking for Charlie in the bunch of kids running and wrestling on the front lawn. Charlie's my favorite cousin; he's always interesting. He lives in Puyallup, which is only about fifty miles away, but we don't see each other real often.

At the last reunion, when I was nine and Charlie was eleven, we had a terrific time until we fell off the barn roof together. I broke my arm and Charlie needed twenty-two stitches. My mother kept saying, "Gracie, how could you have been so foolish?" and my dad said, "That Charlie is going to get somebody killed yet if he doesn't stop doing these harebrained things. How do you stand it, Jim, having a kid that gets into trouble all the time?"

Uncle Jim just laughed. He and Aunt Lila couldn't have any kids—nobody ever explained why—so they adopted three of them. Cissy and Dawn are dark, like the Portwoods, and they're nice little girls. Everybody likes them because they hardly ever cause any problems.

4

And then there's Charlie. He doesn't look like anyone else in the family, and he does cause problems. Uncle Jim and Aunt Lila were so happy to have a son that it didn't bother them when he did things other kids never thought of, like taking a leaky boat out on the river and sinking it with his two little adopted sisters along. The water wasn't deep, but everybody got wet and the girls ruined their shoes.

"He's just being a boy," Uncle Jim said about the incident when we fell off the barn roof.

"But he took Gracie up there on the barn with him," Dad said, "and she's a girl. With a broken arm."

"I'll pay the bills if your insurance company doesn't," Uncle Jim told him, and Dad said that wasn't the point. I never did hear him say what the point was.

Anyway, Charlie was easy to spot in all those Portwoods. He was the only one with bright copper-colored hair. I'd have died to have hair like that, instead of plain old brown. It was not only a beautiful color, it curled.

5

When I got old enough to dye my hair, I intended to have hair exactly like it.

Charlie was on the ground, rolling over and over with Wayne, who was the same age, thirteen. Suddenly Wayne yelled, "Ow! Let go, Charlie, you're breaking my arm!"

"Not again this year," Dad muttered behind me. "Gracie, if I have to spend another three hours in the emergency room with you because of something Charlie talks you into, you're going to be sorry."

"We're all grown up now, Daddy," I told him patiently, and then ran toward the kids.

Wayne was still yelling, and Charlie sat on his stomach, grinning, while my cousin Eddie cheered him on. Wayne often picks on Eddie, because Eddie is small for twelve.

"Hi, Gracie," Charlie greeted me. "Sit on his feet so he'll stop kicking."

I eyed Wayne's size ten Nikes. "I don't think so," I declined. "Do they have any snacks out yet?"

"Peanut butter cookies, apples, and bananas." Charlie suddenly got up, leaving Wayne gasping on the grass. "Let's go get some more, Wayne, before they decide it will spoil our supper. You coming, too, Eddie?"

I tagged along, saying "Hi" to the other cousins who were horsing around or, like Cheryl, standing there watching. Cheryl was twelve, and instead of jeans and a T-shirt she was wearing a skirt and blouse and panty hose, of all things. She came with us, though.

"Everybody's here except Aunt Molly, and she's not coming," Charlie said.

I stopped so short that Cheryl stepped on my heels. "How come?"

"She's bought a house and she's moving into it right away, because the lease is up on her apartment. It's big enough for us to visit, two or three of us at a time. It has a studio where she's going to paint. She said she couldn't move and come here the same week. The new place is within walking distance of Golden Gate Park, so we can go to the zoo and the museum where they have that big gorilla, and the planetarium, and the aquarium."

Aunt Molly was our favorite. She was Mom's youngest sister, even prettier than Mom, and she liked to do all kinds of things the other grown-ups wouldn't do: kick-the-can, sack races, play Monopoly or Clue or Pictionary, swim in the river, build a raft, or go on those rides at the fair that made other adults throw up. When I fell off the roof, she was the only one who didn't think I'd been stupid to be on top of the barn in the first place.

"I broke my arm falling off there, too, when I was ten," she said. And then, to my mother, "Remember, Margaret, I fell on top of you and knocked all the wind out of you so you couldn't even cry at first, and I thought you were dead?"

"And you ran screaming for the house," Mom confirmed, making Dad give her one of those what-can-you-expect-from-a-Portwood looks.

Last reunion Aunt Molly had opened up some trunks in the attic to get out old clothes for costumes, and we'd put on a play she wrote. I was a princess in a pale blue satin gown (that was before I had my arm in a cast) and Charlie was a wicked old villain with a white wig and a sword who kidnapped me; Eddie rescued me with another sword, and we lived happily ever after. What were we going to do this year for entertainment if it rained?

"It's probably just as well Aunt Molly didn't come," Cheryl said primly. "Mama says she's too wild. And she has all those *peculiar* friends. Writers and artists and actors, instead of ordinary people."

I glared at her. "You're still jealous because she chose *me* to be the princess in the play instead of you."

"Well, I was older. More mature."

Charlie made a rude noise. "Gracie was a great princess."

He lunged at me with an imaginary blade, leering. It wasn't quite the same without the costume and the makeup, but he was pretty good. "Now yer in my clutches, me beauty, and I'm going to carry you away forever!"

"Now I suppose we won't see Aunt Molly for another whole two years!" I mourned.

Charlie dropped his pose of villain. "Yes, we will. She called my mom just before we left home, and guess what, Gracie? She's invited you and me and Eddie to go to California and visit her for two weeks, after the reunion. Later some of the other kids will be invited, when she's recovered from us."

"Visit her? In San Francisco?" I'd never been there, but I'd seen pictures from a trip my folks took. The Golden Gate Bridge, the Coit Tower, Alcatraz Island with the famous prison on it. The museums, the cable cars, Fisherman's Wharf, where you could walk around eating shrimp or crab cocktails out of paper cups, and visiting a sailing ship that was over a hundred years old. "Oh, wow!"

And then, even before Cheryl sniffed and said, sounding exactly like her mother, "Oh, who wants to go and visit such a *flake,* anyway," my spirits dropped.

"I don't know if my folks will let me go. How would we get there? Dad says this reunion is all the vacation we're going to get this year except for a week at Copalis Beach just before school starts."

Charlie grinned. "We're going to fly," he said.

"Me, too?" Eddie asked hopefully. Charlie had flown to a lot of places—to visit his other grandparents in Boston, and to Disneyland, and to visit his cousins on the other side of the family, in Atlanta. On that trip he'd gone all by himself, though most of the relatives raised their eyebrows about a twelve-year-old flying alone.

"If your folks will let you go," Charlie confirmed.

I swallowed. "That's the trouble. I don't know if they will. Not if it's just us kids flying."

"Well, don't give up before you ask," Charlie advised. "There's nothing to flying. We get on the plane at Sea-Tac"—that's the Seattle-Tacoma airport—"and then we get off in San Francisco and Aunt Molly meets us. She's even going to pay for the tickets, so nobody can say we can't afford it. It's simple enough. And according to statistics, flying's safer than riding in cars. So why would anybody object?"

I couldn't see any good reason to object, but I was already trying to think up my arguments for when my dad did. It probably wasn't the flying he'd worry about so much as the fact that I'd be traveling with Charlie.

I didn't get a chance to talk to my folks about it until just before we went to bed that night. They had been out for a walk along the river, where they used to go before they were married, and they came back to the house hand in hand in the twilight.

I was waiting my turn for the bathroom, sitting on the edge of the veranda, and I got up and went to meet them. I hoped I could put it right so Dad wouldn't give me a flat no without a chance to discuss it. My stomach felt full of crawly things because I wanted so much for my folks to let me go. I was glad when old Jack got up and tagged along with me, letting me rest a hand on his soft furry head.

"Having a good time?" Mom asked, smiling as I approached.

"Yeah," I said. And then, all in a rush, I told them about Aunt Molly's invitation and the free plane tickets. They looked at each other.

"Well," Mom said thoughtfully, "Gracie is eleven. And she's fairly responsible. If we put her on the plane here, and Molly meets the kids at the other end, what could go wrong?"

"With Charlie heading the expedition?" Dad asked, before I could even begin to feel relieved. "Margaret, your innocence never ceases to amaze me."

He said it jokingly, though, and I began to

seriously hope. "Eddie would be along, too," I said. Eddie never got into trouble, as far as I knew.

Mom looked at Dad again. "What do you think, honey?"

Dad considered for a minute. Old Jack was leaning into my side, so I could scratch behind his ears, almost pushing me over. I braced my legs and held my breath.

"You really want to go?" Dad asked.

"Oh, yes, Daddy! Please, please!"

"I'll tell you what, Gracie. If you can get through this family reunion without being involved in one of Charlie's disasters—no, let me amend that—if we all get through this reunion without there *being* a Charlie-caused disaster, you can go with him and Eddie to Aunt Molly's in San Francisco."

"Oh, Daddy, thank you!" I hugged him, and spun around, racing to find Charlie to tell him the good news.

Dad yelled after me. "But if he pulls another one of his birdbrained schemes, I'm not letting my daughter go off with him anywhere, you understand? Do you hear me, Gracie?"

I turned around to wave acceptance of his terms, then sped toward the house.

Two whole weeks at Aunt Molly's, and flying there by ourselves! What fun!

After all, as Mom said, what could go wrong?

# Chapter Two

Everybody had an opinion about Aunt Molly inviting Charlie and Eddie and me to visit her. Uncle George and Aunt Monica said Eddie could go if I did. I think Aunt Shirley and Uncle Bill were miffed because Wayne wasn't invited first, but everybody else understood *that.* Wayne was always picking on somebody. Just about anybody, except Charlie, who picked on him right back if he started something.

Aunt Joan and Uncle Stan said right off they were glad Cheryl hadn't been invited because they wouldn't have allowed her to go, anyway.

"Why not?" Mom asked when they were all sitting around the big table in the kitchen the next morning, having breakfast. "Just because Molly paints for a living instead of going to an office doesn't mean there's anything strange about her. Molly's perfectly responsible."

Dad was sitting with his back to me, and I guess nobody paid any attention that I was there.

"Maybe Molly is," Uncle Stan said, "but I don't know about Charlie."

Uncle Jim sipped at his coffee and laughed. Uncle Jim laughed about everything, even when Aunt Lila backed the motor home into Grandpa's old pickup that he'd parked behind it when she didn't notice. Grandpa hadn't laughed, but he admitted it was his own fault, because he knew Aunt Lila had backed into things before. "Charlie's very responsible," Uncle Jim said. "He's flown several times across the country by himself, with no difficulty whatever. I got him a credit card, and he handles his own cash sensibly. He's very poised, very mature, for thirteen."

Uncle Bill reached for another doughnut. "Well, I'll tell you, Don," he said to my dad, "with Charlie's record for catastrophes at these reunions, I wouldn't entrust Gracie to him, if I were you."

"We're not exactly entrusting Gracie to him," Mom said. Her face was sideways to me, and I saw that she was a bit annoyed. She had been annoyed with Uncle Bill ever since they were both little kids, because he was always so prissy and so much neater than she was, and she didn't like the comparisons everybody made. "Gracie's mature for an eleven-year-old, too. We trust her to use her common sense, and it only takes a couple of hours to fly from Seattle to San Francisco, for heaven's sake."

"Besides that," Dad said, "I've put a condition on this excursion. Gracie can't go with Charlie unless he gets through this entire reunion without one of his catastrophes." He laughed. "And I'm counting on him not being able to do it."

I felt the heat rising in my face and I knew it was getting red. What a mean plan, I thought angrily. Dad wasn't usually mean.

"Oh, well," Uncle Stan said. "You're probably safe, then."

Uncle Jim shook his head. "Charlie's growing up. You wait and see. He'll be okay this year; no disasters, I can practically promise you."

I decided I'd lost my appetite for orange juice. I went back to the dining room and found Charlie and my little brother, Max, building a tower out of doughnuts while everybody but Cheryl cheered them on. We all held our breaths while Charlie placed the last doughnut on top of the stack and then everybody scrambled to catch them when they toppled and rolled in every direction.

"Listen, Charlie," I said, catching one on the edge of the table and biting into it, "you've got to be on your best behavior this whole week."

Charlie hesitated between a chocolate-covered doughnut and one with colored sprinkles. "Oh? Why?"

"Because my dad says if you screw up and have a catastrophe, I can't go to Aunt Molly's with you. And I want to go."

Eddie looked alarmed. "If Gracie doesn't go, I can't go, either."

Charlie chewed thoughtfully. "What, exactly, constitutes a catastrophe?"

"Something like you usually do," Wayne said. "Falling off a roof, breaking somebody's bones, starting a fire in the hay."

"I was only six when I started the fire in the hay," Charlie pointed out. "I was too young to know better."

"I'm six," Max said. "I know better than to play with matches."

"I did, too," Charlie said, "after Grandpa put out the fire and explained it all to me. Okay, Gracie, no disasters. I'm going to be on my honor not to spoil our trip. Come on, let's go check out the horses."

Everybody went, except Cheryl, of course. You can't ride horses wearing a skirt and panty hose.

It wasn't easy getting through that week.

Most of the time Charlie really tried. It was just that he forgot once in a while that it was important not to get into trouble.

Even Wayne, who had no stake in the trip, tried to help. He caught the pitcher of lemonade when Charlie hit it with his elbow and nearly knocked it off the porch railing into the lilac bushes. Nobody but me saw it.

When Charlie and Eddie were having a rodeo and Eddie fell off old Dusty (Grandpa hasn't used horses to plow since he got the tractor, but he keeps a couple for us kids to ride), I could tell his leg really hurt, but he didn't hightail it to the house for help. He sat in the dirt until the worst of the pain had eased off, and then we rolled up his pant leg and looked at where he'd scraped against a nail that was sticking out of the corral fence.

"How long's it been since you had a tetanus shot?" I asked. I knew about those from having stepped on a nail last summer.

Eddie thought about it, his face still sort of puckered up from looking at the gash. "Two years ago, I guess it was. When I stuck the pitchfork through my foot." He squinted up at me. "Do I have to have another one? I hate shots."

"Tetanus shots are good for ten years," Charlie said. He'd dismounted and was holding the reins on Sister, who wasn't Dusty's sister at all but his mother. "So you got eight more years to go. You didn't break the leg, did you?"

"I don't think so." Eddie looked down, then quickly away from his injury. "It's bleeding."

"I'll go get some disinfectant and a bandage," I said. "You stay here, so nobody will see you."

Charlie gave me a dirty look. "Hey, I didn't throw him off the horse! This isn't part of the catastrophe business, is it?"

"You were playing rodeo with him when he got hurt," I told him bitterly. "And my dad will probably decide that makes it your fault." It still made me mad to think of it, how Dad was counting on my not getting to go.

"Okay. Fix him up. I'll turn the horses back into the pasture," Charlie said. He knew it was my dad I resented, not him.

Luckily the grown-ups weren't around when we went swimming in the river later that day, or Eddie would have had to explain why he had six Band-Aids on his leg. As it was, when his mother asked why he was limping (even though he tried to walk without doing it) he just said he'd bumped his leg, but it was okay. That *was* the truth. Sort of.

It almost spoiled the reunion for me, more or less holding my breath every time Charlie moved for fear something would go wrong. I couldn't figure out what it was, exactly, that made him a menace. He didn't do mean things on purpose, the way Wayne sometimes did. And he wasn't especially klutzy, either.

It was just that when Charlie was around, exciting things happened. And some of them were more exciting than he'd planned. Like the day he showed us how he'd learned to drive and took us for a ride in Grandpa's old pickup. How did he know the brakes were gone? Nobody'd told us.

The truck was so beat up we decided nobody'd notice a few more dents, and we hardly did any damage to the corner of the pig pen. Wayne and Charlie straightened the fence post and propped it up with some big rocks.

That was probably why the pigs got out later that day, but Grandpa just thought they knocked over the post on their own. It was lucky Cheryl wasn't with us in the truck; she's an awful tattletale.

That was why for once I wasn't sorry when the reunion was over. It was a strain, expecting something to happen that would ruin our plans for the trip.

On the last day Uncle Bill asked Dad if he

was still anticipating a reprieve, which I guess meant that Charlie would still mess up. Dad said, "You know Charlie, he's a ticking time bomb."

It made me mad all over again, that Dad didn't really think I'd get to go. So when Charlie offered to show us how he could "tightrope walk" on top of the corral fence, I talked him out of it, just in case he slipped and fell off.

That was the end of the week, and it seemed appealing to go home and sleep in my own bed for a few nights.

And get ready to fly to San Francisco. I could hardly wait.

I had new jeans and a pink knit shirt for the flight.

Dad had gone around saying, "I don't believe that kid actually made it through a whole week without crippling himself or anyone else," but otherwise he was a good sport about losing the bet he'd made with himself. He even got me a flight bag to carry some of my stuff in, besides what I was taking in Mom's medium-size suitcase.

"The flight bag's for a change of underwear and your toothbrush and things like that," Mom said. "Just in case your luggage doesn't match up with you immediately in San Francisco."

"Why wouldn't it?" I asked. "Don't they put it on the same plane?"

"In theory," Mom said dryly. "But I remember the night we spent in Indianapolis once, when we had rushed to change planes and our luggage came on the following flight. That plane was struck by lightning and had to turn back, so our suitcases didn't catch up with us until the following day. We didn't have any clean clothes until twenty minutes before we were supposed to leave the hotel the next morning, when your father was scheduled to make a presentation at a convention. All we had with us was a carry-on bag like this, and we were grateful we at least had his shaving gear and our deodorants." She paused, deciding how many pairs of socks to put into the suitcase. "As I remember it, we really needed the deodorants."

"Okay. I'll take something to read, too, in the air," I said, though I thought I'd probably

ve been viewed historically as alien, different from men, beset by
ductive health problems, and given to psychosomatic and neurotic
aints. Historically, medical treatment of women has frequently
aternalistic and guided by superstition rather than by objective
here is some evidence (mentioned, in part, below) that current
l practice is not yet divorced from past beliefs concerning sex
nces in health.

me of the current drive toward more naturalistic health care,
larly among women, represents a growing awareness of the lim-
of standard medical practice. However, I am also concerned
me aspects of the naturalistic health movement. The message
es seems to be that if you would only adjust your thinking or
right combination of yogurt and vitamins, then health-related
s would disappear. This message, like that in rape, seems to me
ase of blaming the victim. Most people most of the time, in my
are reasonably objective in assessment of their health prob-
ich are more often physiologically based than the current de-
nt of medical diagnosis can reveal. I am not saying that medita-
rcise, and the like, are unhelpful in correcting problems, but
at medicine is simply unable to diagnose and correct many
. And when diagnosis and therapy are unavailable, it may be
eous to the medical professional to define the problem as psy-
ic, for which physicians are not responsible. The naturalistic
vement may unwittingly feed into this attitude.

urpose of this chapter is to examine the potential impact of the
ereotype on health, medical behavior, and medical treatment.
native hypotheses are suggested. The first is that women truly
ter emotional instability than do men so that certain dif-
medical treatment of women and men are warranted, i.e.,
ent prescribing to women of psychotropic drugs such as Val-
endency to ascribe psychogenic illness to women and organi
en. On the other hand, if the differences in treatment are
the operation of certain aspects of the sex role stereotypes
ferences are not warranted and changes need to be institute
education.

## fferences in Health

the most perplexing sex differences in the health field is th
etween morbidity and mortality. Morbidity statistics refle
which persons are required to curtail activities or use dru
lated problems. Mortality statistics present death rates
Although morbidity statistics suggest that women are le
men, mortality statistics suggest the reverse. Men die mo

Maffeo, P. A. Thoughts on Stricker's "Implications of research for psychotherapeutic treatment of women." *American Psychologist*, 1979, *34*, 690–695.

Malchon, M. J., and Penner, L. A. The effects of sex and sex-role identity on the attribution of maladjustment. *Sex Roles*, 1981, *7*, 363–378.

Maracek, J., and Johnson, M. The influence of gender on the process of therapy: A review. In A. M. Brodsky and R. T. Hare-Mustin (Eds.), *Women and psychotherapy*. New York: Guilford Press, 1980.

Masling, J., and Harris, S. Sexual aspects of TAT administration. *Journal of Consulting and Clinical Psychology*, 1969, *33*, 166–169.

Maxfield, R. B. *Sex-role stereotypes of psychotherapists*. Unpublished doctoral dissertation, Adelphi University, 1976.

Munley, P. H. A review of counseling analogue research. *Journal of Counseling Psychology*, 1974, *21*, 320–330.

Parsons, J. E. *The psychobiology of sex differences and sex roles*. New York: Hemisphere, 1980.

Petro, C. S., and Putnam, B. A. Sex-role stereotypes: Issues of attitudinal changes. *Sex Roles*, 1979, *5*, 29–39.

Rice, D. Patient sex differences and selection for individual therapy. *Journal of Nervous and Mental Disease*, 1969, *148*, 124–133.

Schwartz, J. M., and Abramowitz, S. I. Value-related effects on psychiatric judgment. *Archives of General Psychiatry*, 1975, *32*, 1525–1529.

Schwartz, J. M., and Abramowitz, S. I. Effects of client physical attractiveness on clinical judgment. *Psychotherapy: Theory, Research and Practice*, 1978, *15*, 251–256.

Seidenberg, R. Drug advertisements and perception of mental illness. *Mental Hygiene*, 1971, *55*, 21–31.

Sherman, J. A. Therapist attitudes and sex-role stereotyping. In A. M. Brodsky and R. T. Hare-Mustin (Eds.), *Women and psychotherapy*. New York: Guilford Press, 1980.

Siskind, G. Sexual aspects of Thematic Apperception Test administration. *Journal of Consulting and Clinical Psychology*, 1973, *401*, 20–21.

Smith, M. L., Glass, G. V., and Miller, T. I. *The benefits of psychotherapy*. Baltimore: Johns Hopkins University Press, 1980.

Stearns, B. S., Penner, L. A., and Kimmel, E. B. *An experimental investigation of sexism among practicing psychotherapists*. Paper presented at the meeting of the American Psychological Association, Toronto, 1978.

Stein, L. S., Del Gaudio, A. C., and Ansley, M. Y. A comparison of female and male neurotic depressives. *Journal of Clinical Psychology*, 1976, *32*, 19–21.

Stricker, G. Implications of research for psychotherapeutic treatment of women. *American Psychologist*, 1977, *32*, 14–22.

Sue, S. Clients' demographic characteristics and therapeutic treatment: Differences that make a difference. *Journal of Consulting and Clinical Psychology*, 1976, *44*, 864.

Thomas, A. N., and Stewart, N. R. Counselor response to female clients with deviate and conforming career goals. *Journal of Counseling Psychology*, 1971, *18*, 352–357.

Tilby, P. J., and Kalin, R. Effects of sex-role deviant lifestyles in otherwise normal persons on the perception of maladjustment. *Sex Roles*, 1980, *6*, 581–592.

Waldron, I. Why do women live longer than men? *Social Science and Medicine*, 1976, *10*, 349–362.

Weissman, M. M., and Klerman, G. L. Sex differences and the epidemiology of depression. *Archives of General Psychiatry*, 1977, *34*, 98–111.

Werner, P. D., and Block, J. Sex differences in the eyes of expert personality assessors: Unwarranted conclusions. *Journal of Personality Assessment*, 1975, *39*, 110–113.

Wright, C. T., Meadow, A., Abramowitz, S. I., and Davidson, C. V. Psychiatric diagnosis as a function of assessor profession and sex. *Psychology of Women Quarterly*, 1980, *5*, 240–254.

Zeldow, P. Clinical judgment: A search for sex differences. *Psychological Reports*, 1975, *37*, 1135–1142.

Zeldow, P. Effects of nonpathological sex-role stereotypes on student evaluations of psychiatric patients. *Journal of Consulting and Clinical Psychology*, 1976, *44*, 304.

Zeldow, P. B. Sex differences in psychiatric evaluation and treatment: An empirical review. *Archives of General Psychiatry*, 1978, *35*, 89–93.

# Sex Roles in Medicine

## Linda S. Fidell

The extent to which the seeking and receivir
enced by social factors is probably underestir
Although current medical practice has many
it, like the law and education, is still practic
cultural beliefs abound.

For example, although medical diagn
and in many cases may be so, they also rep
labeling of a set of symptoms and signs th
into preestablished diagnostic categories.
are rendered by physicians have consider
implications for patients, depending on t
of perceived illnesses. Rights and oblig
(families, friends, insurance companies,
part, by how a particular set of symptom
symptoms into diagnoses, physicians e>
nomic, and political power (Freidson, 1

For another example, within the n
influence the power and prestige of sp
that the prestige of specialists is related
exerted by the physician over the patie
the physician (e.g., surgeon), the higl
must depend on the cooperation of pa
have lower prestige.

Both Ehrenreich (1974) and Fidell
differences in medical beliefs about m

**Linda S. Fidell** • Department of Psycholog,
California 91330. This chapter is a revised an

en ha
repro
comp
been
data.
medic
differe
Sc
particu
itation:
with s
sometir
find the
problen
to be a
opinion
lems, w
velopme
tion, exe
rather th
problem:
advantag
chosoma
health m
The
sex role s
Two alter
have grea
ferences i
more frequ
ium, or a
illness to
function o
then the di
in medical

## 1. Sex Di

One of
difference b
the extent to
for health-r
age category
healthy than

frequently than women do in every decade starting at birth, yet women have higher morbidity. It is important to identify the reasons for this discrepancy in order to evaluate other sex-related differences in medical treatment.

Several researchers have attempted to explain the discrepancy. Muller (1976) notes that definitions of morbidity are strongly tied to social factors that make the statistics an unreliable index of real health. For instance, the extent to which persons of different sex are asked to curtail activities may reflect more the physicians' expectations about who is more able to curtail activities than who really needs to do so.

Nathanson (1975) offers three models to explain the discrepancy between morbidity and mortality statistics for the two sexes. Explanations include that women merely report more illness consistent with the sex stereotypes, that the sick role is compatible with other roles of women (e.g., housewife) but not those of men (e.g., provider), and that the roles of women are more stressful leading to greater illness. After careful review of the evidence available at the time, she concludes for the second explanation but acknowledges the need for more research. If the second explanation is correct, then as more women enter the labor force, morbidity differences should decline. Have they?

Ortmeyer (1979), in an article I found compelling, argues that the sex mortality differentials increased from 2 years in 1900 to 7.7 years in 1976, as a function of environmental changes rather than biological differences. She points to declining maternal mortality for women versus, for men, substantially higher rates of accidental death and suicide coupled with higher risk from environmental pollutants due to work. Also, she argues that men have been socialized not to admit pain or seek help. According to this analysis, greater mortality among men is not a function of biological differences between the sexes but rather of differences in sex role-related behaviors. Lipman-Blumen (1975) reports that women in high-stress occupations are suffering death rates and stress-related illness rates comparable to those of men in similar positions.

It seems at least plausible, then, to attribute part of both mortality differences and morbidity differences to the operation of sex role stereotypes. How much of medical behavior and medical treatment may be similarly explained?

## 2. Sex Differences in Medical Behavior

### 2.1. Female Patient Behavior

A prevailing belief in the medical profession is that women are more involved with medicine than men and that much of their involvement is unnecessary. Women do make more visits to physicians than do men (58% as opposed to 42%; HEW Publication, 1972). However, both Kravits (1975) and Chien and Schneiderman (1975) report that sex differences in rates of visits to physicians disappear or are substantially reduced when differences in reproduction and the longer life-span of women are taken into account.

But in the process of having greater involvement with the medical profession, women may become at risk of iatrogenic—doctor-induced— illness. That is, women may end up with greater contact with the medical profession because they are made ill by previous contact with it. Steel, Gertman, Crescenzi, and Andrews (1981) report that 36% of admission to a hospital general services facility were iatrogenic, 9% involved a disabling or life-threatening condition, and 2% led to death. Drugs were most frequently involved. Women did not have iatrogenic illness disproportionate to their overall rate of admission to hospital, but more women than men were admitted. Caranasos, Stewart, and Cluff (1974) also found that more white women than black women or men were hospitalized for adverse drug reactions, primarily in persons over 61 years of age. Elsewhere I have argued that misprescribing of drugs has special impact on women for numerous reasons (Fidell, in preparation).

Another interesting explanation for the greater involvement of women with medicine was suggested by a female cardiologist at the Kaiser Permanente Facility in Los Angeles during a Grand Rounds I gave there in 1981. She suggested that women have to seek medical care more than do men because less is known about illnesses that affect women because a primarily male medical research enterprise has concentrated its efforts on the problems that affect men.

Nonetheless, on average, men and women also behave differently during the medical interview, with women presenting a greater number of symptoms with psychological impact. Overall, Kravits (1975) estimates that 12% of the visits to physicians have no physical basis. Women are reported (by physicians) to have 63% of the unexplained symptoms, 61% of the psychiatric symptoms, 60% of the psychosomatic illnesses, and 53% of all diagnosed illnesses. In addition, women may visit physicians more often for psychological or psychosomatic reasons than do men.

In a study of persons recently recovered from rather serious illnesses, Suchman (1972) found that "women were twice as likely as men to report severe symptoms (31% vs. 17%), to view these symptoms seriously (25% vs. 12%), and to become concerned about their importance (51% vs. 42%)" (pp. 160–161). Women were also more likely to have discussed symptoms with other persons prior to deciding to consult a physician but, contrary to expectation, women were less likely than men to contact a doctor immediately (63% vs. 81%). Once receiving care, men and women were equally satisfied with it, although the men were more likely to change physicians independently (23% of women vs. 42% of men). During convalescence, men reported that they were more worried about returning to their prior level of functioning, but they were more likely to say that they were in good health after the illness. These differences in patient behavior are consistent with sex role stereotypes requiring men to be reticent about expressing symptoms but assertive at seeking out alternate health care resources.

Horwitz (1977), in an analysis of events leading persons to seek psychiatric treatment, reports similar sex differences in patient behavior. Prior to visiting a physician, men have most frequently discussed their symptoms with no one, or only with their spouse. Women, on the other hand, are likely to have discussed their symptoms with four or five same-sex friends or kin. By the time women reach the physician's office, therefore, they have much more practice at reporting symptoms and a greater knowledge of likely diagnoses and treatments. Women were also more likely to admit to an emotional component to their illness and to be more optimistic about treatment. I think that the practicing and refining of symptom presentation is of major importance in understanding sex differences in the medical behavior of women and the ultimate impact of these differences on physicians.

Numerous other studies (Clancy and Gove, 1974; Markush and Favero, 1974; Phillips and Segal, 1969) suggest that women tend to report more symptoms than do men and that their symptoms are more likely to have psychological implications than are those of men. There is considerable disagreement, however, concerning the interpretation of these findings. Some ascribe the difference to greater emotional instability on the part of women, whereas others ascribe it to response bias. One of the more convincing explanations is offered by Coser (1975), who points out that since women are trained to be the socioemotional experts in a family, they are expected to monitor and report mental and physical symptoms for both others and themselves. According to this analysis, the greater number of psychological symptoms reported by women reflects sex role learning and not greater emotional disturbance.

## 2.2. Physician Behavior and Expectations

Research involving physicians and their attitudes is generally unsatisfactory because of the difficulty of obtaining a random sample of respondents and because of privileged communication between physician and patient. The small numbers of physicians who do cooperate with a research inquiry are likely, in my opinion, to be more liberal than those who do not respond. The likely direction of the bias would be to minimize sex differences that might occur if a more nearly representative sample of physicians were available.

In a recent small survey, physicians were generally found to be more conservative than lawyers in their notions about the proper role of women, with older physicians more conservative than younger ones (Clingman and Musgrove, 1977). Other surveys have shown that physicians believe women to be more mentally disturbed, to have more social problems and other vague symptoms than men (Cooperstock, 1974). They are also expected to be less stoic than men during illness (Mechanic, 1965).

Further, physicians may expect women to be more difficult patients. Cooperstock (1971) found that when asked to describe "the typical complaining patient"—sex unspecified—72% of the physicians in her Canadian sample spontaneously referred to a woman, whereas 4% referred to a man, and 24% referred to a patient of undetermined sex. As a participant observer, Millman (1977) reports that the words *crock* and *turkey* are used by doctors to identify patients who are likely to give unreliable information. Once the label is applied, the remainder of the patient's remarks are likely to be ignored. "Doctors appear to assign the label 'crock' quite often on grounds of personal or prejudiced responses . . . the label 'crock' also seems to be applied erroneously more often to women" (p. 109).

Mechanic (1970) reports that a physician's level of frustration, harassment, and correlated tendency to believe that patients are presenting trivial, unnecessary, or inappropriate complaints is related more strongly to the number of patients scheduled on a busy day than to the physician's medical background or to other, objective indices of the organization of the practice. "A certain amount of frustration and dissatisfaction is embodied in the personalities and orientations of the doctors themselves" (p. 94). More frustrated practitioners had lower-quality performance on a number of indices, including their drug-prescribing practices, than less frustrated doctors. If doctors were to schedule patients more leisurely, they might simultaneously lower their own frustration levels and improve the quality of service they offer.

Patient sex may influence the prescribing behavior of physicians, as well. Although the prescribing of all drugs is roughly proportional to the rates with which men and women visit physicians, the rates are disproportionate when it comes to the psychotropic or mood-modifying drugs (Fidell, 1981). Steadily over the last several years, women have received over two-thirds of the prescriptions for drugs in these categories. Women are more frequently and more heavily involved than men with the minor and major tranquilizers, the sedative-hypnotics, the stimulants, and the antidepressants. These drugs are usually prescribed by a general practitioner or internist, rather than a mental health expert. Because physicians tend to write a prescription to signal to outpatients that the interview has ended (Muller, 1972), one would expect the sex with the greater number of visits to physicians to receive more prescriptions—but one would not expect the rate to vary by category of drug.

Prescribing practices, however, seem to be strongly related to the attitudes of the physician. Lynn (1971) found that a physician's attitude about the legitimacy of use of minor tranquilizers in a variety of settings is more strongly related to the social values and moral standards of the physician than to his medical or scientific background. The physician who is better educated, holds progressive views, considers the patient as a whole person (Joyce, Last, and Weatherall, 1967), is not authoritarian (Klerman, Sharaf, Holzman, and Levinson, 1969), and finds the patient easy to talk to, if not more likable (Cartwright, 1974), tends not to prescribe mood-modifying drugs. If, on the other hand, the physician is pessimistic about the outcome of treatment or feels anger toward the patient (Shader, Binstock, and Scott, 1968), then mood-modifying drugs are more likely to be prescribed.

From their in-depth study of long-term minor tranquilizer users, Cooperstock and Lennard (1979) report yet another social goal that prescriptions for psychotropic drugs may serve. Women expressed more anger in general toward their physicians than did men and felt that the tranquilizers were, in some cases, used to keep them in a dependent role. Although some of the women who expressed this attitude were seriously ill, they also believed that they were capable of a more adult level of functioning than the one they could achieve with the tranquilizers.

Brodsky (1970) reported that physicians prescribe mood-modifying drugs to housewives in the belief that they can always sleep and need not be mentally alert to perform the job. Lynn (1971) determined that 87% of physicians judge the daily use of a minor tranquilizer as legitimate for housewives, but only 53% consider even occasional use as legitimate for students, with lower percentages viewed as legitimate in all other situations about which opinions were surveyed.

Waldron (1977) provides an excellent review of many other economic and social factors that influence physicians in their prescribing practices for minor tranquilizers. The extent to which prescribing is influenced by considerations other than potential therapeutic benefit is large.

But prescribing in general, and not just that for the psychotropics, is strongly influenced by cultural factors. Lawson and Jick (1976) report striking differences in prescribing patterns for hospitalized patients between Scotland and the United States. Scottish patients receive far fewer drugs and, in turn, suffer less frequent adverse drug reactions. If similar differences were found between the Latin American countries and the United States (with Latin American patients having *more* adverse drugs reactions), the drug companies might be implicated. Silverman (1977) found differences in the indications and side effects listed for the same drug made by the same company promoted in the different countries. In general, the pharmaceutical companies seemed to be revealing as little as legally possible in each country about potential adverse reactions.

Stereotypic notions about women as patients may be reinforced in medical school training, textbooks, and medical advertising. Howell (1974) reported that medical educators teach that women have psychogenic, but not organic, illnesses by shifting the pronoun unconsciously from *he* to *she* when the discussion shifts from organic to psychological illness.

Many gynecological textbooks also perpetuate erroneous notions about women patients, as reported by Scully and Bart (1973), who examined the contents of 27 general gynecological textbooks published in the United States between 1943 and 1972. Most of the texts, even those published after the Kinsey report and the work of Masters and Johnson were widely available, present no information or inaccurate information concerning female sexuality. Many project an image of women as primarily interested in procreation, a view that is consistent with the generally conservative notions of physicians about the proper role of women in society. Luy (1974) gives anecdotal evidence about the treatment that women resent most from gynecologists, some of which may stem from erroneous beliefs about their sexuality taught in medical schools.

With respect to advertisements in leading medical journals, Prather and Fidell (1975) confirmed the tendency to downplay organic illness in women and to portray them as in need of mood-modifying drugs. Women are sometimes shown in advertisements as difficult patients, with the recommendation that a mood-modifying drug be prescribed. Mant and Darrock (1975) reached substantially the same conclusions as Prather and Fidell when they examined advertisements from an Australian medical journal.

## 2.3. Interaction of Female Patient Behavior with Physician Expectations

Numerous studies cited in sections 2.1 and 2.2 suggest that men and women present their symptoms to physicians differently, and that physicians tend to hold stereotypic expectations regarding male and female patients. What happens, then, when the two come together during a medical interview?

Zola (1966) studied the impact of cultural differences on physicians' impressions of patients' presenting symptomology, but his findings are also relevant to the present discussion. His subjects, second-generation Irish and Italian outpatients at an ear, nose, and throat clinic, were matched by equating for final diagnosis. The reaction of physicians to cultural differences in patient style of symptom presentation was examined. Irish and Italian patients behave quite differently. The Irish tend to deny illness, refuse to admit pain, present few symptoms in very specific locations, and state that the illness is not a problem for them or their families. The Italians, on the other hand, are expansive in describing their symptoms, complain of pain, give a large number of symptoms in a variety of locations, and state that their illness is creating problems for them and their families. Physicians react to these differences by asserting that the Irish, who are stoic, suffer from more serious illness than the Italians, who are expansive. And if no organic basis for the complaints is found, the Italians are "diagnosed as having some psychological difficulty . . . whereas the Irish and Anglo-Saxons were consistently given what one might call a neutral diagnosis" (Zola, 1973, p. 686).

Women in this culture may behave more like the expansive Italians, whereas men, in general, act more like the stoic Irish. Mechanic (1972) concludes that boys are more stoic than girls in their medical behavior and that "sex role learning is important in illness behavior and attitudes toward health risks" (p. 131). Physicians may be reacting to sex differences in style of symptom presentation by thinking that women suffer from less serious illness than men.

Bernstein and Kane (1980) varied patient sex and whether or not a patient talked about a personal problem in written vignettes given to physicians. Physicians made more psychosomatic diagnoses for patients of either sex who talked about personal problems. When judging patients who did not talk about personal problems, physicians gave women a psychosomatic diagnosis more often, judged emotional factors as important in the health problem, and expected women to be demanding patients. Note that women were judged to have psychosomatic problems more frequently regardless of whether or not they talked about personal problems, men only when they mentioned personal problems.

Wallen, Waitzkin, and Stoeckles (1979) did a content analysis of 336 actual taped interviews between patients and physicians. They were primarily interested in the explanations given to patients by physicians and whether or not those explanations were appropriate to the level of sophistication (technicality) in the patient's question. Physicians gave the same number of spontaneous explanations overall to both sexes. When the number of explanations given in response to questions was added, physicians gave more numerous explanations to women, primarily because women asked more questions. However, the total amount of time physicians spent explaining was the same for men and women, meaning that spontaneous explanations and explanations given in response to a question were, on average, shorter for women than for men. There was also a tendency for physicians to underestimate the level of technicality of the questions asked by women more often than that for men.

McKinlay (1975) also found that physicians consistently underestimated the level of word comprehension of their lower-class female patients. McKinlay goes on to list several social goals of physicians that may be facilitated if they believe that patients do not understand medically related jargon (e.g., increased efficiency in dealing with hospitalized patients).

An as yet unresearched topic is the interaction of patient nonverbal behavior with physician expectations. Friedman (1979) has pointed to the importance of nonverbal cues of touch, gaze, facial expression, voice, olfaction, and so forth, in the interaction of patient and physician. Although he does not specifically address the question of sex differences, it seems likely that nonverbal behaviors of male and female patients differ, that physicians respond differently in nonverbal ways to the two sexes, and that nonverbal behaviors affect the outcome of the medical interview.

## 3. Sex Differences in Medical Treatment of Men and Women

But what is the outcome of patient differences, physician expectations, and the interaction of the two? Do women, in general, receive the same medical treatment as men or different?

Elsewhere (Fidell, 1980) I have summarized studies that tend to show that certain medical problems (e.g., cardiovascular disease) may be systematically underestimated in women, that changes in certain health-related behaviors of women (e.g., use of estrogen replacement therapy among older women) may be changing risk factors for women, that these changes may or may not have been noted by the medical profession, and that there is ample evidence for sex-stereotypic treatment of women in reproductive medicine.

For instance, certain disorders of female reproduction are thought by physicians to originate psychosomatically, with rejection of femininity as the underlying problem. Thus, Lennane and Lennane (1973) reported that dysmenorrhea, nausea of pregnancy, pain of labor, and infantile behavioral disturbances are seen by the medical profession as having psychogenic etiology. Although scientific evidence exists to the contrary (e.g., in the relationship between prostaglandins and dysmenorrhea), these disorders are often believed to stem from neurosis or attempts on the part of women to use symptoms to escape from ordinary obligations. The logical process used to arrive at this conclusion may represent a reversal of cause and effect. That is, although doctors believe that fear and dislike of menstruation cause dysmenorrhea, it may well be that dysmenorrhea causes fear and dislike of menstruation. Whatever the logical error, however, sympathy is withheld and possibly effective treatment denied a patient who is thought to have psychogenic symptoms.

Armitage, Schneiderman, and Bass (1979) have provided the most direct evidence of sex discrimination in medical treatment. They examined files of husbands and wives in a San Diego practice with several physicians, following complaints of fatigue, dizziness, headaches, chest pain, and low back pain. They created a scale for the quality of work-up received associated with each symptom, and found better and more extensive work-ups for men for each symptom but that of chest pain.

Lack (1980) found that women who had experienced chronic facial pain had received different medical treatment from that of men. The women had received more prescriptions for psychotropic drugs, fewer prescriptions for narcotics, and fewer surgical procedures than had men. The women had also had to search longer and wider for appropriate medical treatment than had the men.

These studies suggest that sex discrimination in medical treatment exists, and that the differences are consistent with the hypotheses suggested in this chapter.

McCranie, Horowitz, and Martin (1978) constructed two symptom and sign profiles, one with headache and one with stomach complaints as the primary symptom. They sent one profile, identified with either a male or female first name and pronoun, together with a booklet containing more information and a set of questions, to 300 general practitioners in private practice in Georgia. The response rate was 117 or over 39%. The physicians did not significantly ascribe psychogenic rather than organic diagnoses to the medical profiles when a woman's name was attached rather than a man's, nor did they rate the illness as less serious. There was a tendency to give a preliminary diagnosis of psychogenic for the women and neurosurgical for the men for the profile describing headache, but the difference did not reach conventional significance levels. This finding, although contradictory with much of the above, is consistent with the general tendency of physicians to give a preliminary diagnosis of illness rather than health (Friedson, 1971; Millman, 1977). Further, evidence that physicians do not bias a *preliminary* diagnosis on the basis of first name in *written* profile, with other patient variables held constant, does not really constitute a test of the ideas presented above.

More disturbing is the report of Verbrugge and Steiner, sponsored by Hoffman-LaRoche, Inc. (1980), who analyzed data from the 1975 National Ambulatory Medical Care Survey and found that medical care in terms of diagnostic services, therapeutic services, and follow-up care is similar for women and men, but when it differs, it is women who get more care, even after statistically adjusting for number of visits and the like. This finding is in direct contrast to that of Armitage et al. (1979), even for the five complaints studied by them. Verbrugge and Steiner suggest that women request more care than do men and show more distress, which prompts sympathetic physicians to greater efforts on their behalf.

What, then, do we make of the contradictions? Verbrugge and Steiner (1980) had a large and presumably representative sample of services performed per visit by sex. The sample was so large, in fact—in the tens of thousands—that many significant differences are to be anticipated even if the percentage of variance accounted for by them are quite small (as most were). But the differences found were in the *wrong* direction for the hypothesis. Armitage et al. (1979) and Lack (1980) both found differences in the predicted direction on much smaller samples (which provide more convincing demonstrations of differences than do very large samples), and in the case of Armitage et al. (1979), very nearly matched groups (husbands vs. their wives). In both these cases, the samples were predominantly middle or upper-middle class, whereas the sample of Verbrugge and Steiner (1980) represented all socioeconomic levels. There may well be class by sex interactions that account for the discrepant findings.

Two very different hypotheses can summarize these data. In the first, women, who are genuinely more neurotic and psychosomatically inclined, visit physicians with trivial complaints. They are given numerous tests, all inconclusive, and finally psychotropic drugs by sympathetic physicians who don't know what else to do. The greater involvement with medicine works to the advantage of women by identifying problems earlier so that women outlive men by several years.

According to the second hypothesis, women, by sex role stereotype and previously practiced symptom presentation, give a more complete list of symptoms to physicians who, perhaps, don't know as much as they should about illnesses that primarily affect women, and who expect women to be more neurotic. Physicians interpret the statements of women as confirmation of their sex-stereotype expectations, and although they order several tests, they dismiss the complaints as psychosomatic and dismiss the women with psychotropic drugs.

Proper scientific incredulity would dictate impartiality between these two hypotheses until evidence is more conclusive, but a recent personal experience indicates otherwise. During a visit to an internist, during which I mentioned several symptoms that seemed, to me at least, to be rather objective evidence of physiological imbalance, after a brief examination, and before any laboratory work, the internist said, "You are a hard-driving woman. It would be easy to dismiss your symptoms as psychosomatic. But I'm not going to do that yet." What evidence exists that "hard-driving" women are more psychosomatically inclined than other women? And if I had been, say, a housewife, instead, would it really have been any different?

# 4. References

Armitage, K. J., Schneiderman, L. J., and Bass, R. A. Response of physicians to medical complaints in men and women. *Journal of the American Medical Association*, 1979, *241*(2), 2186–2187.

Bernstein, B., and Kane, R. *Physicians attitudes toward female patients*. Paper presented at the meeting of the American Federation for Clinical Research, 1980.

Brodsky, C. M. The pharmacology system. *Psychosomatics*, 1970, *11*, 24–30.

Caranasos, G. J., Stewart, R. B., and Cluff, L. E. Drug-induced illness leading to hospitalization. *Journal of the American Medical Association*, 1974, *228*(6), 713–717.

Cartwright, A. Prescribing and the relationship between patients and doctors. In R. Cooperstock (Ed.), *Social aspects of the use of psychotropic drugs*. Toronto: Addiction Research Foundation of Ontario, 1974.

Chien, A., and Schneiderman, L. J. A comparison of health care utilization by husbands and wives. *Journal of Community Health*, 1975, *1*, 118–126.

Clancy, L., and Gove, W. Sex differences in mental health: An analysis of response bias in self-reports. *American Journal of Sociology*, 1974, *80*, 205–216.

Clingman, J. M., and Musgrove, W. J. The attitudes toward women held by practitioners and students in medicine and law. *Sex Roles*, 1977, *3*, 185–188.

Cooperstock, R. Sex differences in the use of mood-modifying drugs: An exploratory model. *Journal of Health and Social Behavior*, 1971, *12*, 238–244.

Cooperstock, R. *Social aspects of the medical use of psychotropic drugs*. Toronto: Addiction Research Foundation of Ontario, 1974.

Cooperstock, R., and Lennard, H. L. Some social meanings of tranquilizer use. *Sociology of Health and Illness*, 1979, *1*(3), 331–347.

Coser, R. L. Why bother? Is research on issues of women's health worthwhile. In V. Olesen (Ed.), *Women and their health: Research implications for a new era* (HEW publication No. (HRA) 77-3138). Washington, D.C.: U.S. Department of Health, Education and Welfare, 1975.

Ehrenreich, B. Gender and objectivity in medicine. *International Journal of Health Services*, 1974, *4*(4), 617–623.

Fidell, L. S. Sex role stereotypes and the American physician. *Psychology of Women Quarterly*, 1980, *4*(3), 313–331.

Fidell, L. S. Sex differences in psychotropic drug use. *Professional Psychology*, 1981, *12*(1), 156–162.

Fidell, L. S. Women, drugs, and physicians. In K. Weiss (Ed.), *Women's health alternative medicine*. Reston, Va.: Reston Publishing (in preparation).

Freidson, E. *Profession of medicine.* New York: Dodd, Mead, 1971.

Friedman, H. S. Nonverbal communication between patients and medical practitioners. *Journal of Social Issues,* 1979, *35*(1), 82–99.

HEW Publication No. (HSM) 72-1074. *Physician visits: Volume and interval since last visit. United States, 1969.* Washington, D.C.: Department of Health, Education and Welfare, 1972.

Horwitz, A. The pathways into psychiatric treatment: Some differences between men and women. *Journal of Health and Social Behavior,* 1977, *18*(2), 169–178.

Howell, M. C. *Women in medical education.* Paper presented at the Annual Meeting of the American Association for the Advancement of Science, San Francisco, 1974.

Joyce, C. R., Last, B., and Weatherall, M. Personal factors as a cause of difference in prescribing by general practitioners. *British Journal of Preventive Social Medicine,* 1967, *21,* 170–177.

Klerman, G. L., Sharaf, M. R., Holzman, M., and Levinson, D. J. *Some relationships between sociopsychological characteristics of resident psychiatrists and their use of drug therapy.* Paper presented at the American Psychiatric Association Meeting, New York, 1969.

Kravits, J. Sex differences in health care: Social survey research methods. In V. Oleson (Ed.), *Women and their health: Research implications for a new era* (HEW Publication No. (HRA) 77-3138). Washington, D.C.: U.S. Department of Health, Education and Welfare, 1975.

Lack, D. Pain differences, similarities found. *Science News,* 1980, *118,* 182–183.

Lawson, D. H., and Jick, H. Drug prescribing in hospitals: An international comparison. *American Journal of Public Health,* 1976, *66*(7), 644–648.

Lennane, K. J., and Lennane, R. J. Alleged psychogenic disorders in women—A possible manifestation of sexual prejudice. *New England Journal of Medicine,* 1973, *288,* 288–292.

Lipman-Blumen, J. Overview—Demographic trends and issues in women's health. In V. Olesen (Ed.), *Women and their health: Research implications for a new era* (HEW Publication No. (HRA) 77-3138). Washington, D.C.: U.S. Department of Health, Education and Welfare, 1975.

Luy, M. L. M. What's behind women's wrath toward gynecologists. *Modern Medicine,* 1974, October, 18–21.

Lynn, L. S. Physician characteristics and attitudes toward legitimate use of psychotherapeutic drugs. *Journal of Health and Social Behavior,* 1971, *12,* 132–140.

Mant, A., and Darroch, D. B. Media images and medical images. *Social Science and Medicine,* 1975, *9,* 613–618.

Markush, R. E., and Favero, R. V. Epidemiologic assessment of stressful life events, depressed mood, and psychophysiological symptoms—A preliminary report. In B. S. Dohrenwend and B. P. Dohrenwend (Eds.), *Stressful life events: Their nature and effects.* New York: Wiley, 1974.

McCranie, E. W., Horowitz, A. J., and Martin, R. M. Alleged sex-role stereotyping in the assessment of women's physical complaints: A study of general practitioners. *Social Science and Medicine,* 1978, *12,* 111–116.

McKinlay, J. B. Who is really ignorant—physician or patient? *Journal of Health and Social Behavior,* 1975, *16,* 3–11.

Mechanic, D. Perception of parental responses to illness. *Journal of Health and Human Behavior,* 1965, *6,* 253–257.

Mechanic, D. Correlates of frustration among British general practitioners. *Journal of Health and Social Behavior,* 1970, *11*(2), 87–104.

Mechanic, D. Response factors in illness: The study of illness behavior. In E. G. Jaco (Ed.), *Patients, physicians and illness.* New York: Free Press, 1972.

Millman, M. *The unkindest cut.* New York: Morrow, 1977.

Muller, C. The overmedicated society: Forces in the market place for medical care. *Science*, 1972, *17*, 488–492.

Muller, C. Methodological issues in health economics research relevant to women. *Women and Health*, 1976, *1*, 3–9.

Nathanson, C. A. Illness and the feminine role: A theoretical review. *Social Science and Medicine*, 1975, *9*, 57–62.

Ortmeyer, L. Female's natural advantage? Or, the unhealthy environment of males? The status of sex mortality differentials. *Women and Health*, 1979, *4*(2), 121–133.

Phillips, D. C., and Segal, B. E. Sexual status and psychiatric symptoms. *American Sociological Review*, 1969, *34*, 58–72.

Prather, J. E., and Fidell, L. S. Sex differences in the content and style of medical advertisements. *Social Science and Medicine*, 1975, *9*, 23–26.

Scully, D., and Bart, P. A funny thing happened on the way to the office: Women in gynecology textbooks. *American Journal of Sociology*, 1973, *78*, 1045–1050.

Shader, R., Binstock, W., and Scott, D. Subjective determinants of drug prescriptions: A study of therapists' attitudes. *Hospital and Community Psychiatry*, 1968, *19*, 384–387.

Shortell, S. M. Occupational prestige differences within the medical and allied health professions. *Social Science and Medicine*, 1974, *8*, 1–10.

Silverman, M. The epidemiology of drug promotion. *International Journal of Health Sciences*, 1977, *7*(2), 157–166.

Steel, K., Gertman, P. M., Crescenzi, C., and Anderson, J. Iatrogenic illness in a general medical service at a university hospital. *New England Journal of Medicine*, 1981, *304*(11), 638–642.

Suchman, E. A. Stages of illness and medical care. In E. G. Jaco (Ed.), *Patients, physicians and illness*. New York: Free Press, 1972.

Verbrugge, L. M., and Steiner, R. P. *Physician treatment of men and women patients—Sex bias or appropriate care?* Paper presented at the American Public Health Association Meetings, Detroit, October, 1980.

Waldron, I. Increased prescribing of Valium, Librium, and other drugs—An example of the influence of economic and social factors on the practice of medicine. *International Journal of Health Services*, 1977, *7*(1), 37–61.

Wallen, J., Waitzkin, H., and Stoeckles, J. D. Physician stereotypes about female health and illness: A study of patient's sex and the informative process during medical interviews. *Women and Health*, 1979, *4*(2), 135–146.

Zola, I. Culture and symptoms—An analysis of patient's presenting complaints. *American Sociological Review*, 1966, *31*, 615–630.

Zola, I. Pathways to the doctor—From person to patient. *Social Science and Medicine*, 1973, *7*, 677–689.

# Index

be too excited about flying to read. I stuck a book into the flight bag, just in case. I knew seasoned travelers *always* carried reading materials.

We met the others at the airport. Eddie had been staying at Uncle Jim and Aunt Lila's instead of going home with his folks after the reunion, and while they were checking in our baggage at the counter, Eddie spoke to me out of the side of his mouth. I thought he'd been watching too many old black-and-white gangster movies.

"It was a close call," he said.

"What was?"

"Charlie fell off a ladder into those glass things Aunt Lila has for her flowers. He made his folks promise not to mention it to Uncle Don."

"That wouldn't have counted against the trip!" I protested, understanding why Charlie had a few nearly healed scratches on his arms and face. "Dad said *during* the reunion, not afterward."

"We weren't taking any chances," Eddie said. "Come on, are you checking that bag?"

"No, I'm carrying it on board in case the other one gets mislaid. I've got snacks in it, too, for if we get hungry and the stewardess doesn't feed us enough."

Eddie nodded. He had a flight bag, too, a bright red one. Mine was light blue with a white stripe. He unzipped his and showed me a bunch of Milky Ways and Almond Joys. "I thought of that, too."

"Listen," Uncle Jim said, resting a hand on Charlie's shoulder, "Cissy and Dawn are due at a birthday party this afternoon, so if it's okay with you, we're going to go on home and not wait for the plane to take off. You don't need us for anything, do you?"

"No, Dad, don't wait. All we have to do is get on the plane when they tell us." Charlie wasn't the least bit nervous, the way I was, just a little. But of course he'd flown before, and I never had. Eddie simply looked excited.

"We'll stay until the flight leaves," Mom said. "We can sit down over there and wait until the plane comes in, all right, kids?"

Sea-Tac is a big airport, and there were hundreds of people, but after Charlie pointed out how organized it all is, it wasn't so scary. We were leaving from Gate 48, and all the information about our flight was posted over a booth, as well as being shown on a television screen with a lot of other flights. Once in a while the information on the TV screen would change, but mostly it said each flight was on time. Except that after we'd sat there for a while and Max was getting tired of watching planes land and take off and wanted something to eat, the passenger agent in her dark blue uniform made an announcement over the loudspeaker.

"Flight 211 to San Francisco will be delayed slightly," she said. "Flight 211 to San Francisco will be delayed."

I jerked. "That's us! Won't we get to go after all?"

"Delayed only means it won't leave quite on time," Dad said calmly. "Sit tight. I'll see what's up."

He wasn't gone long. I was tense, because I didn't want anything to happen to spoil my first adventure on an airplane, my first trip to San Francisco.

"The plane was held up in Salt Lake," Dad told us. "Had a passenger taken ill, it sounded like."

Mom looked at her watch. "Will it take much longer? You told Mr. Hudson you'd be home to accept his call by two thirty."

"Well," Dad speculated, consulting his own watch, "we'll be okay if it's only half an hour or so. Otherwise, if the traffic is heavy, it might be cutting it sort of fine."

"You don't have to stay with us, Uncle Don," Charlie said confidently. "I've done this before, and there's nothing to it. We just sit here where the passenger agent can see us, and when they tell us, we board the plane. We've already got our boarding passes. Why don't you go ahead? No need to miss your call."

"Sure," Eddie added. "We're not babies. We don't need a sitter for an extra half hour of waiting."

My parents hesitated. "Maybe we should go, Don," Mom said. "It's an important call."

"Sure." I put in my two cents worth. "We'll be okay." The adventure wouldn't actually begin until we were on our own.

It was a good thing Dad didn't know all the things *we* knew, or he'd have been more dubious than he was. He was still hesitating.

"We could ask the passenger agent to keep an eye on the kids," Mom said. "There's no question about the plane taking off, is there?"

"No. It'll be here soon! It's on the way. Then it's only a matter of getting it loaded with supplies." His gaze rested on Charlie, who was smiling calmly.

Dad said afterward that he was suspicious of that smile. But I'm sure he wasn't really. If he had been, he'd never have let us stay alone.

"I guess you're right. I'll speak to the attendant," Dad decided.

And then there we were, like seasoned travelers, on our own. I felt like electricity was crackling along all my nerves, I was so excited. It would be the biggest adventure I'd ever had, and I was sure we'd do fine.

I'll have to admit, though, that it wasn't Charlie after all, but me, who took the first step that would change our adventure into a horror story.

# Chapter Three

I was glad Charlie was there, because Sea-Tac is this enormous airport, full of people who acted as if they didn't see us. Eddie put down his flight bag and a hurrying man tripped over it and sent it skidding across the slippery tiled floor. The man never even looked back, let alone apologized.

Eddie rescued the bag, looking uneasy, and sat down again with the bag on his lap.

"There sure are a lot of people going somewhere," he observed as a family group of seven moved past us. They were Asian, loaded with cameras and flight bags similar to ours, wearing shorts or jeans and running shoes. We couldn't understand the language they were using.

Almost as if he were reading my thoughts,

Charlie offered, "It takes about fourteen hours to fly to Japan. Of course they show movies, but that's an awful long time to be fastened in with a seat belt. Dad says it's a good idea to keep your seat belt on even if the sign doesn't say you have to, just in case you encounter turbulence." He seemed to take it for granted that *I* understood that, but he added for Eddie's benefit, "That's when you hit rough weather. If the plane drops suddenly, and you aren't belted in, you could get hurt." And then, to both of us, "On a long flight you get fed quite a few times, though."

He sounded as if he'd been to Japan, but I knew he hadn't.

"Could we go ride on the shuttle?" Eddie asked. That was a sort of little underground train that took you out to the North Satellite, if that was where your flight left from; I'd been on it when we went to meet Grandma Cameron once, and it was fun.

"No," I said firmly. "There's no telling exactly when our flight will leave, and we're not running around taking any chances on missing it."

31

"Yeah, we better stay here," Charlie backed me up, and Eddie sank back in disappointment.

I was getting tired of sitting facing the big floor-to-ceiling windows, because not much was happening out there that we could see. There was a 747 sitting at the next gate over, but nothing was going on over there; nobody was getting on or off. Once in a while, off in the distance, a jet lifted off or landed, but they were only visible for a few minutes.

I shifted around to look back at the people milling around. Two old ladies were having an argument with the passenger agent because the plane was late. We couldn't hear what the uniformed young woman was saying, but the lady with the funny hat was getting quite loud, demanding to know exactly when Flight 211 would take off.

I guess when I turned back around I must have stuck my foot out in front of me farther than I intended, because the next thing I knew a man was falling over it. He lurched forward and dropped the folded newspaper he was carrying as he grabbed at the next chair arm to keep from going all the way to the floor.

I yelped and leaned over to rescue the newspaper, murmuring an apology, but he jerked the paper away from me as if I had some contagious disease. He was rather fat and sloppy, with a wrinkled Hawaiian print shirt and pale blue slacks belted under his belly. His eyes were pale blue, too, and small-ish for his face. My mother would have washed out my mouth with soap if I'd said what he said to me.

I know my face turned red. Charlie made a protesting sound that died when the man snarled at him, too.

I felt awful. People close to us were staring. "I'm sorry," I said again. "I didn't mean to . . ."

I let the words trail off, because he wasn't staying around to listen. He stalked away and took a seat in a back row, away from every-body else.

"What a jerk," Charlie said. "It wasn't like you tripped him on purpose!"

The old ladies who had been making a fuss over the delay went by, giving me disapproving glances. My face burned. I pretended I was interested in a plane that was just landing.

Eddie squirmed on the hard seat beside me. "I'm getting hungry. I wonder if I should eat a candy bar or go buy something. Dad gave me some money. Would I get lost if I went and found something to eat? Do you think the plane would take off before I got back?"

I didn't know if he was really hungry already or only changing the subject to make me feel better.

"Our plane isn't even at the gate yet," Charlie said, standing up and stretching. "It'll come right here when it's ready to load, so we've got plenty of time to get a bite. There's a place down that way, cafeteria style. I'm hungry, too, and we don't want to eat up the stuff we're carrying because we may need it worse later on. Come on, let's go. Bring your flight bags; it's not safe to leave them sitting here." He paused after he picked up his own bag and said under his breath, "What's the matter with him, anyway?"

"Who?" I asked, but I knew, and I didn't turn around quite yet.

"That guy who tripped over your leg. He just gave me a dirty look. He must've been to

34

the islands. Or maybe he's just going there. He doesn't look like he'd have much fun on the beach, if that's where he's going."

"What're the islands?" Eddie wanted to know. For twelve, he was sort of naive. He got his feet tangled up in the straps of his bag before he could pick it up, and then he swiveled around to look past the Japanese family group and an elderly couple talking in whispers. "Wow! You need sunglasses to look at his shirt."

"The Hawaiian Islands, stupid," Charlie said. "Come on."

When I finally turned around, the fat man was reading his newspaper and didn't pay any attention to us. I walked very carefully after the boys, making sure I didn't bump or trip anyone else.

We each got a hamburger and a Coke and Eddie had a bag of potato chips he shared. Eddie eats more for a boy his size than anyone else I know; he was still hungry, but Charlie said maybe we'd better head back to our gate, so Eddie didn't get the second burger he wanted.

We came back down the broad corridor, munching chips. There were more people now. Two planes were loading. It sort of gave me prickles down my spine, because in a short time it would be our turn.

I wondered if it would make me queasy to take off. Charlie had already explained about airsick bags, and I prayed I wouldn't have to use one. I never got carsick, though, so Mom said I'd probably be fine. It would sure be embarrassing if I wasn't.

We were almost back to the seats near our departure gate when it happened.

The old lady walking ahead of us, carrying a light blue bag just like mine, was jostled by an anxious-looking couple running to make their plane, I guess; they knocked her sideways and her purse flew out of her hand and came open, scattering its contents all over the floor.

"Oh, no!" She stopped and half-turned, and I thought she could have been a twin, nearly, to Dad's aunt Letty, who was eighty. She wore plain sensible white shoes and a blue-and-white striped summer dress, with a white sweater over her shoulders.

She stared down with dismay at her belongings, rolling every which way, and someone else came along and kicked a glasses case so it slid under one of the seats on the carpeted area.

"Sorry," a woman muttered when she stepped on a small mirror, but she didn't stop.

The old lady's white sweater had slid off, and I made a grab for it. I couldn't help feeling sorry for her because she seemed so bewildered.

The boys were ahead of me, but I could see the sign for Gate 48, so I knew I couldn't get lost. "Here, I'll help you," I said, and knelt down to reach for the glasses case, hoping none of those hurrying travelers trampled on me while I was retrieving things.

The lady had a nice smile and rather faded blue eyes; she thanked me profusely when I handed her the glasses. "Oh, dear, the mirror's broken, isn't it? Well, I don't believe that old superstition about bad luck, do you? Besides, at my age, seven years of it would be ridiculous."

I picked up the pieces of the mirror. They weren't worth saving, so I dropped them into one of the containers they had for ashtrays. "I think this is all of it," I told her, gathering up a brush with a few silvery hairs clinging to it and a handkerchief with pink roses embroidered in the corner.

She stuffed them back into her purse. "I guess I should have sat down before I tried to open this up for my coin purse. Do I still have that? Oh, yes, here it is." She gave me a wide smile. "You're so kind, dear."

"That's okay." I saw that the boys had stopped and were looking back, and Charlie gestured toward the big windows where a silvery plane stood at our gate. My stomach fluttered with excitement. I was already moving in that direction when the old lady asked, "Can you tell me where Gate Number 48 is, dear?"

"Sure. That's where I'm going. I'll show you," I offered, and hoped she'd walk fast enough so I wouldn't get there late. Our seats were reserved, so it didn't matter for that reason if we weren't at the head of the boarding line, but I wanted to get on and settled as soon as possible. Maybe the butterflies in my middle would subside by the time we took off; they were active enough to make me think uneasily of the airsick bags.

She walked all right. Dad's aunt Letty has bunions, so she walks as if her feet hurt, but this old lady was quite spry. When we entered the boarding area, there was a cluster of passengers around the ticket agent's booth. They weren't forming a line yet, though, and Charlie decided we might as well sit down again rather than stand there holding our bags.

The little old lady sank into the chair next to me with a sigh.

"My goodness, I thought it would be easier than this," she said. "It's such a big place, it's confusing, isn't it? Though I had excellent directions." She gave me a tentative smile. "I'm a little nervous. It's the first time I've ever flown."

Charlie leaned out around me to see her better. "There's nothing to it, ma'am," he said, and I wished Dad could see how polite and thoughtful he was being. "I've flown lots of times."

"Oh, good. My son said it was easy, but he couldn't bring me to the airport." She rummaged in her sweater pocket for a roll of mints, took one, then offered them to us. "Care for a mint?"

We each accepted one and returned the package. She settled back more comfortably, crossing her ankles. "My son drove me up here to visit my sister in Mukilteo, but then he had to go on to Vancouver—the one in British Columbia, not the one in Washington—so I have to fly home alone. My, it's tiring to visit someone for a week." She assessed our looks, seeing us all so different. "You're not brothers and sisters, are you?"

"No. Cousins," I supplied. She'd told us about herself, so I thought I should tell her about us. "We're going to visit our aunt in San Francisco."

"Oh, that's nice. I'm going to San Francisco, too. My daughter-in-law will meet me there. We live in Oakland, actually, so there's a long ride after I get off the plane." She sighed. "Traveling is hard work when you get old. I suppose at your ages, it's an adventure."

"Sure," I agreed, while Charlie was saying, "You get used to it," as if he'd been flying around the world for years.

"Hey," Eddie piped up, "I think they're ready to let us on the plane!" He stood up, looking as excited as I felt, and I was glad I wasn't the only one who wasn't an experienced traveler.

Sure enough, the announcement came over the loudspeaker. "Flight 211 for San Francisco now boarding at Gate 48. Flight 211 for San Francisco."

People got up and began moving toward the door behind the ticket agent. I saw the two ladies who'd made a fuss earlier; they were easy to spot because one of them was wearing a funny red plaid hat, the kind men sometimes wear to play golf.

The rest of us got up, too, and suddenly our new friend exclaimed in annoyance. "Oh, spilling my purse made me forget! I was looking for coins for a newspaper, so I'd have something to read on the plane! I don't suppose there's one of those vending machines right close by—"

She looked around, and I did, too. Charlie shook his head. "No, they're all down that way. I don't think there's time to go and get a paper without maybe missing takeoff."

She looked so disappointed I felt sorry for her. "Well, I guess I'll get by—"

We were heading for the doorway with the other passengers when I saw the newspaper on the chair where the fat man in the Hawaiian shirt had been sitting, at the end of a row of seats. "Hey, look, that man left *his* paper! I'll get that one for you. He must have been finished with it or he would have taken it with him."

I squeezed between the members of another family party speaking a strange language— Charlie said later they were Swiss, though I don't know how he knew—and grabbed the paper that had been neatly folded when the fat man abandoned it. Then, a bit guiltily, because he hadn't seemed to be the sort of person who was generous with strangers, I scanned the people in line ahead of us. Maybe he'd left it accidentally and would resent my picking it up.

He wasn't in the line, though, nor anywhere behind us, either. That shirt would have stood out even in all these people. "Here," I said, handing over the newspaper to the old lady.

Again she thanked me sweetly. "That's very thoughtful of you. This will make the time pass more quickly." She handed over her boarding pass and moved ahead of us, through the doorway onto the sloping carpeted corridor that connected with the plane. We relinquished our passes, too, and followed.

"San Francisco, here we come!" Eddie said with enthusiasm.

I was a little nervous, but mostly I was delighted to be going. I'd have plenty to tell my friends when I got home two weeks from now, and for once when we had to write in school about how we'd spent our vacation, I'd have something interesting to say.

I never dreamed just how much there would be, or I'd probably have turned around and got off the plane before it ever left the ground.

Or maybe not. Mr. Frost raised his eyebrows when he read my paper, and asked how much of it really happened. But he gave me an A+ on it, so maybe it was worth it.

# chapter four

A smiling stewardess in a smart navy blue uniform welcomed us aboard. People were clogging up the aisle as they paused to store carry-on luggage in the overhead compartments. Some of them were confused about where their seats were, but Charlie led the way to ours as soon as we could get through.

I heard Eddie, behind me, mutter an apology as he bumped his flight bag into someone. "Who wants to sit next to the window?" Charlie asked, stopping at our row.

I wanted to, but Eddie had already said breathlessly, "I do!" before I could get my mouth open.

"Okay. You sit there going down and Gracie can have the window seat coming home. I'll sit in the middle," Charlie said. It stood to reason

Charlie would make the decisions. He always did, though he often gave in if you argued.

Eddie slid in first, awkwardly stowing his flight bag under the seat ahead of him before he half-fell into his own place. His glasses had gotten bumped, and he settled them back on his nose as Charlie took the middle seat, leaving me to the one on the aisle.

We were on a 727, and there were three seats on each side of the aisle. I settled into a comfortable seat and grinned. We were finally going!

Of course we didn't go immediately. Though the plane wasn't quite full, there were probably ninety or a hundred passengers who had to load. The old lady we'd met in the waiting area turned out to be right across the aisle from me. She nodded, pleased.

"It looks as if we're going to travel together, doesn't it? I never introduced myself. I'm Clara Basker."

I told her my name, and Charlie's and Eddie's. There was an empty seat beside Mrs. Basker, and she looked at it hesitantly. "I wonder if I can keep my purse there, or if I'll have to put it on the floor? I'm always taking my glasses off or putting them back on, depending on whether I want to read or not, and I'd like to keep them handy."

There was a young woman in the window seat beyond Mrs. Basker, holding a sleeping baby. "Just put it there for now," she suggested. "It's Jimmy's seat, but I have to hold him for takeoff and until he wakes up, anyway."

I heard them exchange names—the young woman was Eleanor Hall—and then turned to look past Eddie to where luggage was still being loaded from a cart out on the concrete area. Charlie was already fastening his seat belt, so Eddie and I followed his example.

I was glad I'd sat on the aisle, after all. The seats had high backs so it was hard to see the people behind or in front of you. But I could lean out into the aisle a little and see quite a bit.

People were making themselves comfortable. Some of them already had pillows and were getting ready for naps. I'd never felt less like a nap in my life. I wasn't even bored, as Charlie obviously was, when one of our three stews, as Charlie referred to the flight attendants, stood at the front of the plane and explained how to fasten seat belts, and where the exits were, and what to do if we lost oxygen and had to use the masks that would automatically drop down. I'd never heard any of it before. She didn't explain about airsick bags, so I hoped that meant we wouldn't be likely to need them.

When the engines came on, Eddie leaned out to see around Charlie and gave me a look of pure delight. "We're going!" he said.

We didn't move for several minutes, however, and after a bit of time had passed I heard a few comments from other passengers.

"What's the delay now? We're already late, and I've got a connection to make in San Francisco."

"Probably waiting our turn at a runway," someone else said.

We realized why the additional delay had been necessary when a flustered-looking man in crumpled slacks and a tan shirt suddenly came aboard, handing over his boarding pass. They must have held the plane for this late passenger, because immediately the engines got louder, and the entrance door was closed and secured.

The man looked down the aisle, his gaze sweeping over me, then settling on Mrs. Basker. "Can I sit there?" he asked the stewardess.

"I'm sorry, Mr. Upton. That seat is reserved for a young child; he's sleeping now, but he will be sitting there later. You've been assigned to 12D. That's right here."

The latecomer scowled, and I felt sorry for the attendant. He looked disagreeable and he was still standing there.

"I'm sorry. Please take your seat, sir, and fasten your seat belt so that we can take off. As you know, we're already behind schedule."

"Yeah," came a voice from behind us, "for pete's sake, sit down so we can take off! You're going to make me miss my connection to Miami." Mr. Upton gave the speaker a surly look and dropped into his assigned seat ahead of us, on the aisle. I could see his foot sticking out where someone could trip over it, about a size twelve in brown oxfords. His pants slid up far enough so I could see he was wearing funny-looking socks. Argyles, I think they're called. His were sort of a brown and green plaid. Then he got settled and drew in his feet and I couldn't see anything but a sort of hairy arm sticking out beyond the back of his seat.

"We're moving!" Eddie breathed, and I forgot about Mr. Upton who was so late he nearly missed the flight.

My stomach got a tight feeling, and my fingers curled around the arms of my own seat. I glanced at Mrs. Basker and saw that she was looking a bit tense, too, but she smiled at me, and I smiled back. It was a first flight for both of us, and I didn't want her to think I was chicken. Mom says showing you're scared makes other people scared, the way I did when I screamed my head off the time Max got hit in the face with a ball and bled all over his shirt front. He wasn't badly hurt, just scared, because *I* acted as if he'd been killed. As soon as I stopped yelling, so did Max. So I made an effort and relaxed my hands. I couldn't do anything about my stomach, though.

We taxied out to the runway, moving slowly at first, and then the engines built to a roar, and we were actually on the runway. Charlie was relaxed, but I noticed Eddie's knuckles were white, even though he was grinning.

We just barely felt it when the plane left the ground. We were lifting, lifting, and it was a rather lovely sensation, I told Mom later. We went up and up, and the plane tilted to one side so we had a view of bright blue water—Puget Sound—below us, and then we circled around and headed south.

A minute later, the FASTEN SEAT BELT sign went off. I heard several people around me exhale, so I figured I wasn't the only one who'd been holding my breath. Some of them unfastened their belts, but Charlie left his buckled, so I did, too.

"Geez," Eddie said with satisfaction, "that made me hungry. I think I'll have a candy bar."

When he leaned forward to reach his flight bag, Charlie gave him a poke with an elbow. "Don't waste your own stuff. They'll bring us a snack in just a few minutes."

This turned out to be true. The attendants brought a little cart along the aisle and asked what we wanted to drink. Eddie had Coke, and I ordered 7-Up. Charlie looked the stewardess right in the eye and said, "I'll have a martini, I guess."

I saw Eddie's scandalized face, and then the stewardess laughed, and I knew Charlie was joking. She gave him 7-Up, like mine.

I knew Uncle Jim sometimes drank martinis, but I was relieved to know he didn't let Charlie have them. My dad would probably kill me if he thought I even sat next to a kid who was drinking anything alcoholic. Especially if the kid was my cousin Charlie.

They gave us little bags of salted peanuts, too. They were pretty good. Mrs. Basker said she couldn't chew them very well so she passed hers across to me, and I shared it with the boys.

Ahead of me, the late-arriving passenger, Mr. Upton, got out of his seat and started toward the back of the plane where the rest rooms were. Instinctively I shrank toward Charlie so he wouldn't brush against my arm as he passed.

He didn't touch me, but one of his big feet caught in the straps of Mrs. Basker's flight bag, which were sticking out from under the seat ahead of her. He actually dragged it along with him, as if he didn't feel it, until I said, "Excuse me, but you're caught on that bag—"

He turned around then, and Mrs. Basker made a grab for her bag. He had to lift his foot to be free of it, and he muttered, "Sorry." He didn't look sorry, though. He had a sour-looking face, and for some reason, I thought he didn't like me, though I couldn't imagine why.

"I'd better tuck it farther under the seat," Mrs. Basker said. "First, though, I'll find my glasses and the newspaper and read a bit. Would you like the comics, dear?"

I took them, though I was still feeling too unsettled to want to read. We hadn't seen the day's funnies from the *Seattle Times,* though, so we all read them.

To my surprise, Mr. Upton paused beside my seat when he came back. "Excuse me, ma'am," he said to Mrs. Basker, "but could I read your paper when you're finished with it? I didn't have time to buy a copy before we took off."

"Oh, why, I don't know," Mrs. Basker said

uncertainly. "I've already promised it to someone else after I finish with it."

I caught only a glimpse of his face—he
didn't seem to like *anyone*—and then a man a
row back said, "Here, I'm finished with mine.
Take it."

Mr. Upton hesitated, then accepted the
newspaper handed over by the other passenger.
"Thanks," he grunted, and returned to his seat.

I really wouldn't have cared if Mrs. Basker
had given the man the paper. I'd already read
the comics. When she finally handed over the
rest of the paper though, I noticed there was a
crossword puzzle. The fat man in the Hawaiian
shirt had filled in a few of the spaces but not
enough to spoil it. I decided I'd finish it if I got
bored, though I wasn't bored yet. I folded the
paper back together and stuck it in my own
flight bag.

My grandma Cameron got me started
doing crosswords the time she stayed with
us after she fell and broke her hip. All she
could do was read and watch TV and do
crosswords, and she kept asking me things
like what was a four-letter word for teutonic

land ownership (Dad knew that word was "odal") or a nine-letter word for the terminal outgrowth of the tarsus of an arthropod. I figured that one meant something that grew out of the end of something, but I didn't know what either tarsus or arthropod meant, so she made me look them up. The answer was "pretarsus," not a word you'd ever use in ordinary conversation.

At first it was sort of aggravating when she kept asking me these words I didn't know—after all, *she* was the one who was the crossword expert, and if she didn't know, how did she expect *me* to?—but after a while I got sort of hooked on learning new words. So maybe I'd do the puzzle before we got to San Francisco.

Eddie had brought a pocket chess set. He got it out and set up the board with the magnetized pieces, and he and Charlie started a game. There was no way three of us could play chess, and it's not the most exciting thing in the world to watch a chess game, so I talked to Mrs. Basker.

When Mr. Upton walked to the back of the plane for the third time, Mrs. Basker stared after him in concern. "Poor man. I wonder if he has a kidney problem. Even I don't have to go to the bathroom that often."

"He's certainly clumsy," Mrs. Hall said. "He manages to trip on your flight bag every time he goes past."

Mrs. Basker looked distressed. "Oh, my, I've tried to tuck it securely under the seat. I wouldn't want him to get hurt by tripping on it." She bent over and shoved the bag as far away from the aisle as she could reach.

Mr. Upton had just come back to his seat when the FASTEN SEAT BELT sign came back on, and a little bell sounded to call attention to it. A moment late the captain spoke over the public address system.

"Please fasten your seat belts, ladies and gentlemen. I regret to tell you that we must make an unscheduled stop in Portland. There is nothing to be alarmed about, and we will make every effort to see that Flight 211 is resumed as quickly as possible. If you have a problem with connecting flights in San Francisco, please consult the passenger agent as soon as we land. Thank you for your patience."

There was a buzz of conversation around us.

"I thought we didn't stop anywhere except in San Francisco," Eddie said, looking up from the chess board.

"He said an unscheduled stop, stupid," Charlie said. "I bet I know what it is!"

Someone behind us raised his voice. "If this means I miss my flight to Dallas, I'm going to be very angry. Stewardess, what does this mean? Why are we landing? I only have fifteen minutes to get to my connecting flight as it is!"

The stewardess shook her head. "I'm sorry, sir. I don't know any more than you do. Excuse me, I must prepare for landing. I'm sure your questions will be addressed as soon as we're on the ground." She moved away, and the buzzing voices continued around us.

"Engine trouble? Do you think it could be engine trouble?"

"Aunt Sophie will have kittens if our plane is late. She'll think something dreadful has happened to us."

"Planes are late all the time. We were late taking off from Seattle, remember?"

"If we get a tail wind, maybe we can make

up the lost time. Don't worry about it, Gladys. We'll handle it when we get there."

Charlie's eyes were shining. "I'll bet I know," he whispered.

"What?" I asked automatically. I didn't see how Charlie could know if the flight attendants didn't know.

It was as if Charlie read my mind. "They wouldn't tell us, because they don't want to panic the passengers."

Eddie's eyes were huge. "What? What is it, Charlie?"

"I'll bet," Charlie said, keeping his voice low so it wouldn't carry beyond the three of us, "that terrorists have planted a bomb aboard!"

# Chapter five

For a minute I thought Eddie was going to choke.

"Are we being hijacked?"

"Of course not," I said quickly. "Hijackers would be waving guns around, demanding to be taken to Cuba or somewhere like that." But my heart was beginning to pound.

"A bomb threat," Charlie repeated. "I'll bet you anything."

"Maybe someone's up there, in First Class," Eddie said, gesturing toward the forward compartment. "With a gun."

I leaned out into the aisle to see. "I don't think so. Two of the stewardesses are standing in the galley or the buffet, or whatever they call it. They're laughing. They wouldn't be laughing if we were being hijacked."

"Or if there was a bomb on board, either," Eddie said, looking reproachfully at Charlie.

Charlie was undaunted by this logic. "They don't *know* yet, that's all. Probably only the crew in the cockpit know. That's where the radio is. All they've told the flight attendants is to buckle themselves in, preparing to land."

"Anyway, we're going to land in Portland," I observed. We felt the change in the plane as it began a turn, and then quickly began to descend.

"You're so full of baloney, Charlie," Eddie told him, "I never know when to believe you. There's no way you could know, any more than the stewardesses, what's happening."

Charlie smiled a small, secretive smile. "You wait and see," he said.

Around us other passengers were speculating on why we were landing, but none of them seemed to have as much imagination as Charlie. Mostly they were concerned or angry about the possibility of missing connecting flights.

"If we're on the ground very long," I said, "maybe we'd better call Aunt Molly and tell her we're going to be late."

"Sure," Charlie agreed. "No need to tell her why. It would only upset her."

"I just hope my mom doesn't call her to see if we got in right on time," I mused, trying to relax. The jet angled down, down, and it made my stomach feel peculiar. "If we get into any kind of trouble, it may be the last trip my folks ever let me take."

"What kind of trouble would we be in," Charlie asked reasonably, "just because our plane made an unscheduled stop? It's not our fault."

"Besides," Eddie added, "it may just be that a passenger is sick, or there's an important passenger they want us to pick up in Portland. Something perfectly simple."

It was clear that he was less thrilled than Charlie was at the idea that we might be landing because of a bomb scare.

Charlie shook his head in condescending amusement. "You're so naive, Eddie. You wait and see. I'll be right."

Eddie shifted his gaze to me and I shrugged. As the jet banked I caught a glimpse of the Columbia River below us as we dropped rapidly into Portland International Airport, and my stomach was tightening up again.

We landed without a hitch, of course. I felt it when the wheels touched down, but it was smooth and easy. I heard Mrs. Basker exhale in relief and figured she'd been holding her breath, too. She gave me a nervous smile.

"I suppose one gets used to this, after a while," she said, almost in apology.

"Sure," I agreed. "I wonder, are we supposed to take our stuff with us when we get off? Or will we be getting right back on?"

"If we're picking up someone, or letting someone off who's sick," Eddie said hopefully, "we shouldn't have to get off ourselves, should we?"

Charlie rolled his eyes. "Why won't you believe me?" he asked.

Charlie was right about the getting-off part of it. As soon as we'd rolled up to the gate, even before the FASTEN SEAT BELT sign went off, one of the attendants made the announcement.

"We do not expect to be in Portland for more than a short time, but the captain asks that you take your carry-on baggage with you when

61

you leave the plane. It is suggested that you remain in the boarding area. The passenger agent will keep you informed as to when Flight 211 will resume. We apologize for any inconvenience and thank you for your patience."

"What patience?" Mrs. Hall muttered, but she didn't sound angry about the delay.

A few other people did. We unfastened our belts and scrambled around getting our carry-on luggage amid some grumbling. Our exit from the plane was slowed by people asking questions of the flight crew, questions nobody was answering.

Mr. Upton was just ahead of me. As sour as he'd been when he boarded, I expected him to be pretty grumpy about an unscheduled landing; after all, he'd had to rush and almost missed the flight, so I figured it was important to him to get to San Francisco in a hurry. However, he shuffled along with everyone else, in no particular rush now.

Mrs. Basker was right behind me. She seemed perfectly cheerful. "I wonder if the delay will mean we won't get our dinner as scheduled? I called ahead to see if they would be serving a meal, or if I should plan on a substantial lunch before I left, and they said we'd have dinner. If that's canceled because of whatever this problem is, maybe I'd better try to get a bite while we're here. I wonder if they can tell us how long it will be?"

They couldn't. Everybody was wanting to know the same thing, but the stewardess at the door could only smile and shake her head. She didn't know yet. And if the captain had informed her of why we'd had to land, she wasn't sharing the information with the passengers.

"Getting a snack sounds like a good idea," Eddie said, though since it had only taken us about an hour to fly to Portland, his hamburger and chips had barely had time to settle.

"Yeah," Charlie agreed. "Let's find out first if they'll announce departure from here over the P.A. system. If so, it should be safe to go find a place to eat."

We went up the carpeted ramp, being jostled by anxious or disgruntled travelers. Mrs. Basker had somehow gotten ahead of us, and I recognized her voice. "Excuse me, sir, I think you've gotten caught on my bag."

I glanced up to see her disentangling the straps of her flight bag from Mr. Upton's hand, which seemed to have snagged on it as they walked side by side up the ramp.

"Oh, sorry," he said, letting her pull it free. "It's so crowded in here, you can't help walking on each other."

I didn't think it was *that* crowded. Since Mr. Upton hadn't been carrying any luggage when he boarded, I didn't see how he could have confused her bag with one of his own, or how he could have failed to notice when he'd caught on hers, but it was none of my business. At least he wasn't snarling at her, though he looked annoyed, the way he had when the stewardess had refused to allow him to change seats.

There was a crowd milling around the passenger agent's booth, but they did at least tell us that the P.A. announcer would give us enough warning to get back for our flight.

Portland International was pretty big, too. (Charlie, naturally, had to inform us that San Francisco International was much bigger. I thought it might be nice to travel somewhere

Charlie hadn't already been, so he didn't know *everything* ahead of the rest of us.)

We trotted across garish red-and-blue carpeting in Charlie's wake. "There's a Häagen Dazs ice-cream parlor down this way," he informed us, and I thought maybe it was a good idea, after all, that he knew the way to *that*. Eddie and I would have been hesitant to get that far away from our plane for fear of getting confused on how to get back fast when our departure was announced.

There were huge murals on the walls of the city of Portland and of the rocky Oregon coast. We hurried along, bags slapping against us, past a display of a really old-style car that looked brand-new—Charlie said it was built from a kit, so it wasn't a genuine antique—and other displays of sculptures and a model airplane. Eddie wanted to pause at that last one, but I nudged him.

"You want time to eat, or not? You can look at that on the way back if there's time."

Reluctantly, he drew himself away. "Yeah. An ice-cream shop, Charlie said. Maybe a banana split would go good."

That sounded good to me, too. I dodged around a potted plant—some kind of miniature palm tree—and looked ahead down the wide corridor. "They've got signs in Japanese," I noted. "And banks and clothing stores, even."

"Expensive," Charlie said succinctly. Of course I hadn't intended to buy anything there; like Eddie, I was only looking.

We all three had banana splits. They were expensive, too, but huge and delicious. When we finished there still hadn't been any announcement about Flight 211. On our way back to our loading area, the boys both checked out the model airplane again.

There was a confectioners' and we investigated the prices of their chocolates, then decided we'd stick with the candy bars we had. There were candy places in San Francisco, too, and we didn't want to run out of money before we even got there.

I saw a bank of telephones and stopped. "I forgot, I was going to call Aunt Molly. Here, Charlie, hold this while I find her number. I hope she's home. I wouldn't want her to call Mom when we don't show up on time, just to see if we left when we were supposed to. Dad would have the F.B.I. on the case in half an hour."

I shoved my flight bag at Charlie and dug into my purse for the phone number. I was lucky; Aunt Molly answered on the second ring.

She sounded startled when she recognized my voice. "You're not here already, are you, Gracie?"

"No. We had to land in Portland for some reason, and we're going to be late getting to San Francisco."

"Oh. Engine trouble?"

"They didn't tell us. Charlie's sure terrorists put a bomb on board."

Aunt Molly laughed. "Sounds like Charlie, all right. Have they given you any idea how late you'll get here?"

"Not so far. And I suppose by the time they do, there won't be time to call you back."

"Well, let's see. I'm not keen on sitting at the airport for hours waiting, but I don't want you to have to wait, either. Tell you what. Have you got something to write with? And a piece of paper?"

"Just a minute." I found a pencil but no

paper except the newspaper Mrs. Basker had handed me. I'd use the edge of that. "Okay. Shoot."

"Take down this phone number." She read it off, and I read it back to her to make sure I had it right. "This is my friend Andrea's number, and she lives only two miles from the airport. I'll wait at her apartment, and then it won't take long when you call for me to get there. Let me know as soon as you get in, before you go to collect your luggage, all right? Then I'll meet you in the baggage area. I should be there by the time you've claimed your suitcases. If you don't see me, wait by the Avis counter; they have a red sign, so it's easy to see. You got that?"

"Got it," I agreed.

"Good. I'll be waiting for your call. See you in a few hours," Aunt Molly confirmed, and we said good-bye.

When we got back to the loading area, we recognized a lot of the passengers waiting there. Including one that surprised us quite a bit.

I grabbed Charlie's arm. "Hey! Look! It's

the crabby guy in the Hawaiian shirt, from Seattle! He didn't get on Flight 211, did he?"

"No way," Charlie said, swiveling to stare at the man, who hadn't noticed us. He grinned. "He followed you to get back his newspaper."

"How'd he get here the same time we did? Well, no more than half an hour later, anyway."

"Who knows? He's witchy enough he could have come on a broom."

"He must have taken a later flight," Eddie said, more practically.

"Or he chartered his own plane," Charlie suggested.

The man in the Hawaiian shirt seemed to be looking over the crowd from a vantage point on the edge of it. He was chewing gum like crazy. I began to understand why our teachers wouldn't let us chew it in class; he looked gross.

"Why would he do that? He could have flown on our plane; there were empty seats, and he was there in plenty of time to get on it," I objected.

"He probably had to go to the bathroom at the last minute and didn't get back fast enough, so he missed the flight."

"We got delayed while we waited for that other guy," Eddie pointed out. "He'd have had to be in the bathroom for a long time."

Charlie laughed. "That's been known to happen. Maybe there was a long waiting line or something. Come on, let's find seats. It doesn't look as if we're leaving soon."

The seats close to the departure door were taken, so we settled down in a back row. I was arranging my bag and purse under my seat when I heard the conversation ahead of us, between a couple I remembered had been angry and upset about the delay.

"How will we know it's safe to get back on the plane?" the woman was asking.

"Gladys, they won't let us on unless it's safe."

"But if they don't find the bomb, how will we know it isn't still on there?"

I sucked in a breath and sat back, forgetting my gear. A bomb?

"If they don't find it, it's because there *is* no bomb," the husband replied. "So it will be safe to get on the plane. I promise you."

"How can you know that, Howard? Why

would anyone tell them there was a bomb aboard if there wasn't one?"

"Who knows why kooks do things? They like a good laugh, knowing they scared a whole lot of people, I suppose. The security people are used to things like this, Gladys. Trust them to take care of it. They won't take any chances loading up a plane if there's any possibility there's a bomb hidden on it."

I looked at Charlie. He was grinning. Eddie's mouth had sagged open so he looked a bit like Max's goldfish.

"I told you," Charlie said, sounding smug. "A bomb."

So Charlie was right again. I sighed.

Of course it never occurred to any of us that a bomb threat had anything to do with *us*. Not even to Charlie.

# Chapter Six

Charlie was right. There was no question about it. We had landed in Portland because of a bomb threat.

I wondered if it would be in the paper, and imagined what my dad would say. I didn't see how they could blame this on Charlie, but it wouldn't surprise me if Dad did.

Everybody was talking about it. Charlie struck up a conversation with the man beyond him, who seemed to know all about it.

"Did the passenger agent make an announcement about it?" Charlie wanted to know.

"No, no. The airlines don't tell you anything. But we saw the crew going on board to search the plane, and somebody talked to one of *them*. Seems like there was a phone call—up in Seattle, where the flight originated—said there was a bomb aboard, set to go off over San Francisco. Some of those idiots protesting something by trying to kill off a whole planeload of people! What good's that going to do their cause, whatever it is?" The man was middle-aged, rather overweight and bald, wearing a rumpled business suit. He sighed. "The crew's been in there and gone, and they still aren't letting us get back on. Oh, ho, they're bringing in reinforcements! See, there's another crew going on!"

It didn't seem to me they'd leave the plane as close as it was to the terminal if they really thought there was a likelihood it would blow up, but of course it wasn't scheduled to be over San Francisco quite yet, though we'd already been in Portland for over half an hour. We watched the new crew of investigators go aboard; and as soon as they'd disappeared down the carpeted ramp, the buzz of excited conversation started again.

The woman in front of us spoke in agitation. "Howard, I'm not getting back on that plane, not unless they carry a bomb off and I see it! I want to change our reservations to another airplane!"

"They're not going to carry it off so we can see it even if they find one," her husband told her crossly. "They'd put it in a steel box or something before they handled it. Besides, the chances are there is no bomb. Just some kooks getting their kicks by scaring people and causing a ruckus."

"I want you to see if you can get us on another plane," Gladys insisted.

"There isn't another plane for two hours. By that time, they'll have put us back on this one."

"But what if it's not safe?"

I didn't like Gladys's voice, she was so whiney, but I could sympathize with her. I felt pretty uneasy about getting back on a plane that might have a bomb on it, too.

Charlie must have read that in my face. He shook his head. "There's no way they'll endanger ninety or a hundred passengers without being sure. Don't worry. If they aren't sure, they'll send us on a different plane. When one's available."

The woman named Gladys heard him and turned around, stricken. "You mean there might not be another one available? We might not get to San Francisco tonight? I mean, our plane was almost full. They can't get all of us on the *next* plane along with the people who've already reserved seats on it!" She didn't wait for Charlie to respond, but turned to her husband in dismay. "What will Julie think if we don't show up for her wedding?"

"We'll show up. They'll get us there," her husband said, and by now he was speaking through his teeth. "I'm gonna go get a cup of coffee. You coming or you want to sit here and work yourself into a stroke?"

She went with him, but she continued to worry in a voice that carried across the waiting area.

Mrs. Basker passed them, saw us, and came toward us with a rueful smile to sit down beside me. "It's rather exciting, isn't it? You read about such things in the papers, but you don't expect it will happen on *your* flight. I guess they haven't found the bomb yet?"

"No. Another crew just went aboard a few minutes ago. Where did you hear about it?"

"Oh, everybody in the restaurant was talking about it. They try to keep such things quiet, but everybody knows. I thought I'd go have a sandwich, in case they don't have time to serve us dinner when we finally get back in the air. I had a patty melt. I'd never heard of them before, and I felt adventurous. Have you ever eaten one? It was quite good, though I suppose it had too much cholesterol."

I nodded. "Did you hear anything about how long it might take them, before we take off again?"

"I don't suppose they'll know, unless they find a bomb. But I'm sure it will be all right. My, my son thought I would be bored by my first flight, but it hasn't been a bit boring, has it?"

"Not really," I admitted, and hoped my parents would be as calm about it as this old lady was.

We sat there for another ten minutes, and nothing seemed to be happening. I saw the man in the Hawaiian shirt lounging by a pillar at one side of the waiting area and wondered guiltily if he'd gone back for his newspaper after I'd taken it. Maybe that was why he'd missed our flight and had to take a later one. I hoped, in that case, that he didn't know I had the paper.

The bomb squad was still on the plane.

Nobody made any announcements. Suddenly Mrs. Basker spoke to me.

"I think I'll go to the rest room one last time before we board. And I'll get some cough drops; my throat feels a bit scratchy. I wonder, would you mind watching my sweater and this box of chocolates I got for my son and his family? I couldn't resist them. It's so awkward, carrying a sweater, and it's too warm to wear it."

"Sure," I told her. "I'll watch them."

She placed the parcel and the sweater carefully on the seat beside me and walked away. I hoped nobody else ran into her and knocked her purse open again. I noticed that the man in the Hawaiian shirt had decided to take a stroll, too, as had several other people. Everybody was tired of sitting still.

Mrs. Basker had been gone probably ten minutes, and Eddie was debating whether or not to add to his food supply before we took off again when one of the airline employees picked up the microphone at her booth. I poked Charlie with my elbow. "Maybe we're finally going to go!" I looked around for Mrs. Basker, but she was nowhere in sight.

"Passengers for Flight 211 to San Francisco," the attendant said, her voice sounding metallic over the speaking system, "your attention, please. Flight 211 will resume in approximately thirty minutes. You will be boarding a different aircraft, at this gate, in thirty minutes. You are urged to be ready to board with your carry-on baggage at that time. For those of you scheduled to make connecting flights in San Francisco, consult our passenger agent immediately for assistance."

We checked our watches. Half an hour, and on a different jet. I felt a bit relieved. "I suppose we'll never know if they actually find a bomb," I said.

"Sometimes they put it on the six o'clock news," Charlie commented. "At least we're not going to have to sit here all night. I was beginning to wonder."

Eddie rustled a candy bar wrapper as he opened it. "What would happen if we had to stay here all night? Would we just sit here in these uncomfortable chairs?"

"No, they'd send us to hotels," Charlie assured him. "They even pay for them, and your dinner if you have to eat in a restaurant. Well, if we've got half an hour, why don't we walk down to that model display? If I've got any money left in two weeks maybe I can find something like them before we leave San Francisco."

"I can't go," I said, when both boys stood up. "Not unless I carry Mrs. Basker's stuff. I told her I'd watch it."

Charlie frowned. "How long's she been gone? She didn't hear the announcement. Maybe we better find her and tell her when the new plane is leaving. Anything is better than sitting in this chair any longer."

We ended up with Eddie carrying the box of chocolates and me stuffing Mrs. Basker's sweater into the side pocket of my flight bag with the newspaper I hadn't gotten around to looking at. When we left the seating area, it had worked out that I would go into the ladies' room to find Mrs. Basker, and the boys would go take another look at the models on display farther along the corridor.

There were a dozen or so women in the rest room, but none of them was Mrs. Basker. I even called her name, and looked under the doors for a pair of feet in sensible white shoes. She wasn't there.

Well, she'd said something about cough drops, too. I pushed through the heavy door and walked along to the gift shop. She wasn't there, either.

Frowning a little, I joined the boys, who were trying to decide which models they would buy if they had the money.

"Find her?" Charlie asked absently. I saw that they'd each acquired a package of corn chips.

"No. Nowhere."

"Maybe she went out another door or something, and back to the boarding area," Eddie offered through a mouthful of chips.

But when we got back there, with fifteen minutes to spare, there was no sign of Mrs. Basker.

"Now I'm getting worried," I said, hoping I didn't sound like the woman named Gladys.

"She's not your responsibility," Charlie said.

"I've got her sweater, and Eddie has her candy. That makes us sort of responsible. What are we supposed to do if it's time to take off and she hasn't come back yet?"

"She's a grown woman," Charlie pointed out.

"She's an *old lady,*" I countered. "Like Grandma or Aunt Sophie. And this is the first time she's ever been in an airport. If she were Grandma, wouldn't you want someone to look after her, if she needed it?"

Charlie gave me a resigned look. "Okay. What do you want to do?"

"Look for her," I said, glad he wasn't going to make me go by myself.

We walked the length of the main corridor nearest our gate, looking into every business establishment, even the places like the bank and the bars. There was no sign of Mrs. Basker.

In the gift shop I asked the clerk, between customers, if she remembered an old lady in a blue-and-white striped dress, who had bought cough drops.

The girl nodded. "Yes, I remember her. She bought cherry cough drops and a magazine. *People,* I think it was."

"We think she's lost. Would you have noticed which way she went when she left here? Maybe she got turned around and walked away from our boarding area instead of toward it."

"The man she was with seemed to know where he was going. They went that way." The girl gestured, away from our boarding area.

"A man? She was with a man?" I asked, puzzled. "She's traveling alone."

"What did he look like?" Charlie put in.

The clerk thought a minute. I suppose it was a miracle she remembered anything about Mrs. Basker, considering the number of customers she'd waited on. "Just an ordinary man. About forty, forty-five, maybe. I think he was wearing tan slacks and a sport shirt about the same color. I'm sorry, I really can't remember any more than that. Excuse me, I have to wait on these customers."

"A man," I said blankly, turning away from the counter. "Why would she have gone anywhere with a man? She intended to come right back; she knew the plane would be leaving pretty soon." I checked the time again, and saw that it was running out, yet how could I leave it at this? "What if something happened to her?"

"Like what?" Eddie wanted to know.

"If I knew *what,* I wouldn't still be wondering. Look, I know it's getting late, but I'm going to take a quick walk down that way and see if there's any sign of her. If there isn't, I guess we'll just have to give her stuff to the passenger agent and explain she's supposed to be on our plane and we don't know what happened to her. Maybe she got sick or something—though if she was with a man, and seemed to be all right when she left the gift store . . ."

My voice trailed. If she hadn't looked so much like Dad's aunt Letty, or somebody's grandma, or she hadn't asked me to watch her things, maybe I wouldn't have bothered. But the truth was, I *did* feel somewhat responsible.

"Well, come on, let's hurry up," Charlie said, "or we'll miss the plane, and then your dad will finally have a real reason to think we're irresponsible."

"It isn't Gracie he thinks is irresponsible," Eddie informed him as we half-ran along the corridor amid a group that had just come off a plane, lugging bags and bundles. "It's you, Charlie."

"Thanks a heap," Charlie told him good-naturedly. "She's nowhere in sight, Gracie, and we're getting farther from our gate all the time. We've got to turn around and go back."

He was right. If we didn't turn around within the next few minutes, we'd have to run to make it. I could imagine sitting in front of Gladys and Howard and listening to her complain about our delaying the rest of our trip—if they didn't leave without us, that was.

To our right a stairway rose to a third level, and there was a sign that said RESTRICTED AREA; NO ADMITTANCE. Charlie saw me looking and shook his head.

"She can read. She wouldn't have gone up there."

"No," I agreed, and turned reluctantly to retrace our steps.

And then I saw it. A blue-and-white flight bag, just like mine, stuffed halfway into one of those refuse containers with a swinging lid on the top of it.

I stopped, and a cold feeling swept through me.

"It's hers," I said, sounding hollow. "It's Mrs. Basker's flight bag. Why would she throw it away? Charlie, something's happened to her, and we've got to find out what it was."

# Chapter Seven

Eddie stared at the discarded flight bag. "How do you know it's hers? You've got one just like it, Gracie, and I've seen some other ones the same color, too. They sell them everywhere."

"It's Mrs. Basker's," I said with certainty. I pulled the bag out of the trash container and unzipped it. "Look! It's got her glasses in it, the same case I picked up off the floor! She'd never have thrown away her glasses!"

"No," Charlie agreed. "Maybe somebody snatched the bag and took what they wanted out of it, then threw it away. She's probably looking for it, or went to find the security guards to report it." He looked up and down the corridor, but though there were lots of people, there was no old lady in a blue-and-white striped dress.

"We've got to catch our plane in only about ten minutes," Eddie reminded us. "We better just take her bag to a security person and take off. Let them handle it."

I supposed he was right—we weren't cops, after all—but I couldn't help being worried about Mrs. Basker. "What if she got hurt or something when the guy stole her bag? She'd probably fight to keep it."

I looked up the stairs that led to the third, forbidden, level. "What do you suppose is up there?"

"Offices," Charlie said at once. "I think the security headquarters are up there, too. There's no reason to think she's up there, Gracie. The signs say 'no admittance' and you don't see any traffic on the stairs, do you? There's nothing to say the cops are up there, either, so why would she go up there?"

"I don't know. But there's something on the steps—"

I shrugged off his restraining hand and ran up the off-limits stairway, snatching up what had from a distance looked like a dropped paper napkin. It wasn't a napkin, though.

"This is hers!" I exclaimed, spreading out the handkerchief so they could see the embroidery in the corner. "I picked this up, too, when she spilled the stuff out of her purse!"

For once Charlie didn't waste time arguing about an idea just because it hadn't been his in the first place. "Come on. I guess we've got time for a quick check. Maybe a security guard took her up to the offices to make a report or something."

We ran up the stairs. Between Mrs. Basker's things and our own, we had about all we could carry. When we reached the third-floor level, I was breathing heavily, and it wasn't all from the climb. I had a really anxious feeling about what had happened to Mrs. Basker.

The longest corridor I ever saw ran off in both directions. There were no people around, and it was very quiet compared to the rest of the airport. There were open doors showing that workmen were remodeling or building, but no workmen.

"Geez, guys, we haven't got much time," Eddie said uneasily. "What if we miss the plane? Everybody will be mad at us, and what if they make us pay for new tickets on another flight? We haven't got enough money for that." He licked salt from the corn chips off his lips. "If anybody's folks have to drive down from Seattle to pick us up, we're going to be in trouble for sure."

I knew he was right, but I didn't take time to discuss it. "I'm going to open some of these doors and see if I can find anybody who saw her."

"You and Eddie go that way," Charlie suggested. "One of you take each side of the hall. I'll go the other way. There's a sign that says 'security office' down that way. If nobody finds her, we'll tell the guards we have to catch a plane in a few minutes. Then they can take care of it."

Eddie and I fairly flew along the hall, opening doors, calling out into unfurnished and unfinished rooms. We didn't have to go very far.

The sign said AIRLINE PERSONNEL ONLY. Some of the doors had been locked, but Eddie twisted this knob and shoved inward, and a moment later his yelp brought me back to him.

"You were right, Gracie," he said, his eyes practically bulging out of his head. "I think . . . I think she's been murdered!"

For a minute, staring past Eddie, I was afraid he was right.

The room was some sort of lounge that didn't look quite finished; there were tarps down where someone had been painting the walls, and a ladder and paint cans.

What we looked at, though, was Mrs. Basker. She was lying on her side on the floor so that we couldn't see her face, but the blue-and-white striped dress and the comfortable white shoes were unmistakable.

I sucked in a painful breath. Was Eddie right? I pushed past him—he stood frozen, blocking the doorway—and dropped to my knees beside the old lady. The straps of my flight bag slid off my shoulder, and something crunched under my weight, objects I recognized.

I'd picked some of them up earlier, when her purse had been knocked out of her hands and spilled on the tiled floor.

"It looks like somebody grabbed her purse and emptied it out," I said, sounding choked, which was the way I felt. And scared. I was definitely scared.

So was Eddie. His Adam's apple was bobbing up and down and he couldn't even talk until his second try. "Is she . . . dead?"

I never took anybody's pulse before, but I'd seen it done in the movies. I felt around on her wrist until I found it. "She's alive, but I think somebody hit her on the head. See, there's a big purple bruise. Run, Eddie, get Charlie and the cops, and tell them to call a doctor, or an ambulance!"

Only after Eddie had fled did it occur to me that I was alone here with an unconscious old woman and that the person who hit her and robbed her might still be around. I'll bet my own pulse was beating a mile a minute. "Mrs. Basker," I said urgently, "can you hear me?"

She didn't answer me, didn't move. I swallowed hard. Please, please, don't let her be dead, I thought.

And then, aloud, I said, "Hurry up, Charlie! Come with the cops!"

I suppose it didn't really take very long. Charlie ran, so he got there first, but the security officer was right behind him. A second officer peered in the doorway and immediately started speaking into the walkie-talkie he unclipped from his belt, calling for a medic team.

Things were sort of a jumble then for a few minutes. The officers asked questions, and we tried to answer them. Charlie was the one who finally remembered our plane was probably already leaving. The second officer said, "Don't worry about it, we'll have them hold it for you," and got on his little radio again.

Two men came with a stretcher and lifted Mrs. Basker onto it and took her away. They picked up her belongings and said they'd see that she got them. Her wallet and change purse were still there, with money still in them, and her identification.

The officer counted through the bills. "Hmm. A hundred and six dollars. Doesn't look as if robbery was the motive. Unless you kids scared him off before he had a chance to get it. Do you know if she was carrying anything else of value? Jewelry, maybe?"

I shook my head. "I don't think so. She spilled her purse before we left Sea-Tac, when somebody ran into her. I picked the stuff up, and didn't see anything like that."

"Anything missing, that you can notice?"

I looked at the accumulation of brush, comb, Kleenex—all the odds and ends a woman carries in her purse. "No," I said. "Not that I can tell."

"Well, we've got your names and addresses, and the phone number where you'll be in San Francisco," he said finally. "Let's get you on to your flight. Someone will probably want to talk to you later, if they have more questions."

"Maybe whoever did it is still hiding in one of the rooms along this corridor," Charlie said. "Maybe you ought to search the whole third floor."

The officer regarded him the way people often looked at Charlie. The way my dad looks at him. "Actually, we thought of that," he said dryly. "My guess, though, is the guy left here long before you kids found her. He stuffed her flight bag in the trash at the foot of the stairs, right? Searched through it up here after he'd knocked her out, found what he wanted in it— or gave up when he didn't find it—and got rid of it down there. So he's well away from here by now."

I guess that was supposed to make us feel safe to go back to our departure gate, but I couldn't help looking around for someone dangerous all the way there, even with Charlie and Eddie and one of the security guards with me. The trouble was, I didn't know what a dangerous person would look like. He could be anyone.

Just before we reached the boarding area, which was practically empty now—everybody else was apparently already on the plane—I remembered something. "The clerk in the gift shop saw her with a man, she said. It must have been the one who hit her, don't you think?"

The officer's interest quickened. "That so? The gift shop near the stairs? I'll talk to her, see if she can give me a description of him. Though he's probably long gone, now. Out of the airport, and beyond jurisdiction. The regular police will handle it from here on."

"What about Mrs. Basker? Do you think she'll be okay?" I wondered.

"Well, she was knocked out, but she didn't

seem to have a depressed fracture or anything like that. I'm not a doctor, but I think she'll probably come around all right. Probably have a bad headache for a few days. Here you go, lady, these are the last of your passengers," he said to the waiting passenger agent. He had a parting word for us. "It'd be better if you don't talk too much about this, except to your parents. The news people have a way of blowing everything out of portion, and there's a lot we don't know yet."

"Sure," Charlie said, and Eddie and I murmured our agreement.

Everybody looked at us as if we were some weird species of bug under a microscope when we finally boarded the new plane. I felt very self-conscious being stared at by a whole planeload of people. I couldn't blame them for being curious, but I sort of resented the comments from Gladys and Howard behind us. (We took the same places as we'd had on the first plane.)

"I don't see why we had to wait for *them*, just because they're kids," Gladys observed in a tone loud enough for us to hear. "We've already been delayed so much we'll just barely make it to the wedding."

"Inconsiderate," Howard said, finally finding something he and his wife could agree on. "That's the way kids are these days. Never think of anyone but themselves."

My cheeks felt hot as I fastened my seat belt. It wasn't fair to say that when he didn't have the slightest idea what had happened to us, or to lump all kids together in the way they behaved.

Mrs. Hall leaned forward across the empty seats beside her. "Do you know what's happened to the lady who was here before? Mrs. Basker? She was supposed to be going on to San Francisco, wasn't she? I mean, we weren't even scheduled to *land* in Portland."

"She got hurt," I said, after a moment of hesitation. "She's been taken to a hospital."

Mrs. Hall drew back, shocked. "Really? Oh my, how did it happen?"

Charlie nudged me warningly, and I resisted the impulse to tell the whole story, as far as we knew it, to let Gladys and Howard know how wrong they were about us.

"We don't know exactly," I told her. "Only that she hurt her head."

Mrs. Hall made clucking noises, but I didn't volunteer any more. Maybe, by some miracle, our names wouldn't be mentioned if any of this got into the paper. I could see my dad reading it and demanding that we return home at once, even before we'd seen anything of Aunt Molly or San Francisco.

This time I wasn't nervous about taking off. In fact I was so busy thinking about poor Mrs. Basker, and hoping she would be all right, that I was barely aware of the plane leaving the ground. What had her assailant been after? She didn't look like a person you'd expect to be carrying a lot of money or any other valuables. I couldn't help wondering how much difference it would have made if we'd gone with her to the restaurant for sandwiches instead of having banana splits.

When I mused about that aloud, Charlie, as always, had an instant reply. "We'd probably have been knocked over the head and robbed, too. Gracie, are you sure you didn't see anything in her stuff that somebody might have wanted? Important-looking papers, something valuable? I don't buy the idea that the guy was scared off before he could take her money; it was right in plain sight. I think he was after something else."

"Like microfilm," Eddie suggested. He was already eating again, another candy bar. I wondered why his teeth didn't rot out, and why he wasn't fat instead of skinny. "Maybe she's a spy."

"Oh, for pete's sake," I said. "They don't have seventy-year-old women for spies, Eddie."

"Why not?" Charlie asked, just when I thought maybe he and I on were on the same wavelength. "They'd be less suspicious-looking than anyone else."

"She wasn't a spy," I said crossly. "She was just a nice old lady taking her first airplane trip. And I didn't see anything that looked like microfilm or suspicious documents. Of course I didn't see what she had in her flight bag, but it probably was only a change of underwear and her toothbrush."

"Maybe the loot from a bank robbery,"

Eddie said thoughtfully, crumpling his candy wrapper. "She could have been a member of a gang, and they had her take the money because she looked the least suspicious, and then she double-crossed them."

Charlie laughed, but I didn't. "You're an idiot, Eddie," I told him, and lapsed into silence. My cousins were too silly to talk to.

I was very much aware of Mrs. Basker's empty seat across the aisle. I hoped she wasn't seriously hurt.

Well, it was all over now, and she was being taken care of. We had nothing more to worry about, I thought.

That was until I got up to go back to the rest room a little while later and saw something that made me start doing some serious thinking.

Because when I stood up I saw there were a couple of people already waiting to use the rest rooms at the rear of the plane, and two of them were the unpleasant man in the Hawaiian shirt and Mr. Upton. They had been talking to each other, only when they saw me they pretended they hadn't been.

And it suddenly struck me that Mr. Upton fitted the description of the man the clerk in the gift shop had seen with Mrs. Basker.

It was suspicious enough to make me suddenly very much afraid.

# Chapter Eight

I sat down suddenly, no longer wanting to visit the rest room, at least not while those two men were standing at the rear of the plane. My breath gushed out of me like somebody'd hit me in the stomach.

"What's the matter?" Charlie asked.

I felt the way I do when I have to stand up in front of class and recite something I was supposed to have memorized—when I wasn't sure I wouldn't go blank in the middle of it.

"Did somebody else disappear?" Eddie asked, trying to be funny.

I gave him a look that told him how funny I thought he was, which was not very. "They're both on the plane," I said in a low voice. "The guy in the Hawaiian shirt and the one who boarded late in Seattle, Mr. Upton. They're standing outside the rest rooms back there, talking, only when they saw me looking they pretended they weren't."

"So?" Eddie asked, his forehead wrinkling up.

I could tell by Charlie's face that his thoughts, however, were taking the same track as mine: suspicion.

"Mr. Upton," I said with lips that felt sort of numb, "is wearing tan slacks and shirt. And he's about forty, wouldn't you say?"

Charlie put it together at once. "The man the clerk in the gift shop described," he said.

Understanding finally washed over Eddie's face. "The man with Mrs. Basker, before she disappeared?" He shoved his glasses higher on his nose. "You think he's the one who did it? Attacked her and robbed her?"

"You're slow, Eddie, but you get there," Charlie told him kindly. "I guess it's time to do some detective work."

"Let's tell the stewardess, so they can arrest Mr. Upton when we get to San Francisco," Eddie said eagerly.

Charlie's gaze was withering, and even I knew better than that. "And tell her what?" I asked. "What's our evidence? Our proof? The police aren't going to arrest anybody on our say-so, without proof!"

"But the clerk described that Upton guy! That's enough to take him in for questioning, isn't it?"

"What good will that do?" Charlie said. "Unless there's some real evidence? All he has to do is say he doesn't know what we're talking about. Or that he spoke to Mrs. Basker about something perfectly innocent, like she dropped a coin and he picked it up and handed it to her. It would be his word against ours, and figure out who they're going to believe. As long as she's unconscious, Mrs. Basker isn't going to accuse him of attacking her. We didn't *see* him do anything to Mrs. Basker or even speak to her."

"The guy in the Hawaiian shirt followed her when she left her stuff with us," I said, finally remembering. "She walked away and when I turned around to look at her, he was heading in the same direction."

"But it was Upton—if that's really his name—she was seen with in the gift shop,"

Charlie mused. "And now they're both on this plane, talking together and pretending they weren't when you saw them, which means they're probably in cahoots, right?"

"Right," Eddie and I said in a chorus.

"We talked about it before," I added, "only then it didn't seem particularly important, and now it does. The Hawaiian-shirt guy didn't fly with us from Sea-Tac, but he showed up in Portland only a little while after we landed there. He sat around in Seattle for at least half an hour before our flight left. If he was coming here, why didn't he get on that plane?"

"Maybe he was only going as far as Portland," Eddie said, "and Flight 211 wasn't scheduled to land there, remember?"

Before I had decided that Eddie had, for once, said something sensible, Charlie asked, "Then why is he now on the plane to San Francisco? This gets fishier and fishier. There wasn't another plane to Portland or San Francisco on that TV screen schedule, not on our airline or our gate. I read it several times to see if anything had changed while we were sitting there waiting."

"Then how did he get here?" I demanded in a fierce half-whisper. "Why would he take another airline after he'd sat there as if he were waiting for *our* flight?"

"He could have gone on an errand and missed the flight," Charlie said, thinking it out as he went, "or he could have changed his mind about going until it was too late. And then he decided he had to go, after all, and—and chartered a plane, I suppose. Those small planes don't fly as fast as the jets, but we were on the ground in Portland for quite a while before he showed up, weren't we? Time enough for even a small plane to have made it."

I was dubious. "Doesn't it cost an awful lot to charter a plane?"

"Not necessarily. Sometimes it doesn't cost any more than regular airline tickets. Besides, if it was really important, the cost might not matter to him."

"Like," Eddie ventured, "if they were gang members who robbed a bank, and Mrs. Basker double-crossed them and took off with the loot, and they had to chase her."

"Oh, Eddie," I said in exasperation, "this is

serious! Try to think of something *logical,* will you? She sat right there in front of Hawaiian shirt, and he didn't do anything, did he? Do you think she'd have sat talking to us—or he would have ignored her—if she'd been stealing their stolen money?"

Eddie didn't give up. "Probably he didn't want to knock her over the head while there were people watching. He had to get her alone, like luring her up onto the third floor in the Portland airport, where nobody could see what he did."

"Well, he knew she was getting on Flight 211—that was obvious—so why didn't he get a ticket and come on that plane, then? Why charter another plane after she'd left the ground? He had plenty of time in Sea-Tac to do that. Besides, Mrs. Basker wouldn't have stolen anything from anyone. She's a perfectly nice woman. She wouldn't be mixed up with bank robbers or spies or any such types."

"She's mixed up with something, though," Charlie said thoughtfully. "We've got to figure out what it is. Then maybe we'll have the evidence to take to the cops so they can arrest those guys. What do we know about Mrs. Basker, besides the fact that she was flying to San Francisco?"

"She drove up to Seattle to visit her sister," I provided promptly, "with her son. He had to go on to Vancouver, B.C., on business, so she's flying back alone. That's it."

"I wonder what her son's business is? Maybe she's carrying something for him. Not stolen money," Charlie added quickly, as Eddie's face lit up with a new looney-tunes idea, "but maybe he's in some high-tech industry and he gave her specifications for computer chips or the like. Foreigners are always anxious to steal American technology, see how it works, and make it without paying for the ideas, then sell it cheaper than Americans can sell it."

"You sound as crazy as Eddie," I scoffed. I really needed to go back and use that rest room; I wondered if those two men were still back there.

"Well, there had to be some reason why the guy hit her over the head, searched her purse, didn't find what he was after, grabbed the flight bag to search later, and threw it away after he'd gone through it. Either he found what he wanted or he didn't, but it's a pretty sure bet the guy was looking for something specific, and it wasn't money, or he'd have taken that out of her wallet." Charlie screwed up his face, thinking about it.

"She's just an ordinary old lady," I said weakly, but there was no denying that what had happened to her had been extraordinary. "Listen, Charlie, come back to the rest rooms with me. I don't want to get near those guys by myself."

"They're not going to knock you over the head here, in front of a planeload of people," Charlie said, but he was already unbuckling his seat belt. "We've got from here to San Francisco, gang, to figure this thing out. If we don't, those jerks are going to get away with whatever it was."

"I wonder if even Mrs. Basker knew what they wanted," I said, sliding out of my seat again. "I can't figure why she'd have gone into that restricted area with one of those men."

Eddie never gave up. "Maybe they dragged her there. Or drugged her coffee when she had lunch, so she passed out, and they pretended they were taking care of her."

I expected Charlie to explode that one, but he didn't. He paused in the aisle behind me to reply. "Maybe you're right. She didn't seem foolish enough to go with them voluntarily."

Eddie pried open his seat belt and scrambled after us. "I'll go with you, too. I don't want to have to go back there by myself later. Just in case those guys are dangerous."

As we walked past Gladys and Howard, I heard the woman sniff. "Kids! Always making up crazy stories, thinking they're spies or private detectives or something!"

"It's all that TV they watch," Howard agreed.

For a minute I wished we *were* making it all up, that it wasn't real. But when I walked past Hawaiian shirt and Mr. Upton—who weren't sitting anywhere near each other—I knew it was real, all right.

I could practically feel the danger oozing out of them, toward us.

Mr. Upton never glanced up from the paper he was reading, but Hawaiian shirt gave me a look that sent prickles of apprehension up my spine. If the boys hadn't been with me, I don't know if I'd have had nerve enough to walk past him. He was seated on the aisle, and I almost brushed against his arm as I went past.

Nothing happened, though, for the rest of the flight. The attendants served us another snack in place of the dinner we were supposed to have had. I tried to read my book and couldn't concentrate on it. The boys didn't even play chess or talk much. I guess we were all trying to figure out the mystery.

One thing was no mystery. Once we landed, those men were going to get away with it, whatever they had done. There was nothing definite we could report to the police, only our suspicions.

And the whole time, thinking about Mr. Upton and Hawaiian shirt behind us, I kept feeling the short hairs on the back of my neck rising up, just the way they do in horror stories. Only this wasn't imagination, I thought. And it wasn't fun, because I couldn't put the book away, or turn off the TV, and go find Max or Mom and Dad to talk to until I forgot the scary parts.

When the FASTEN SEAT BELT sign came on, and the plane banked and circled around to make its approach to San Francisco International Airport from the south, we had a marvelous view of the Bay Area. Passengers around us exclaimed over glimpses of the Pacific Ocean, and Golden Gate Bridge, and the bay, looking bright blue and sparkling in the late afternoon sunshine. Even the city itself looked golden and magical.

Excitement stirred again as I thought about the two weeks ahead of us with Aunt Molly. I knew it was going to be wonderful, and I'd have all kinds of things to relate to my friends when I got home.

It wasn't until we were off the plane that things started to get frightening again, when we found out that it wasn't over yet, the series of events that had begun in Sea-Tac when I helped Mrs. Basker pick up the spilled contents of her purse.

It was in San Francisco Airport that we finally figured out what those men wanted, though we still didn't know why.

# Chapter Nine

I didn't mean to look toward the rear of the plane when we were gathering up our things to leave. It was almost as if I felt an unfriendly gaze on my back and just *had* to turn to see.

Sure enough, they were both looking at me, though Mr. Upton immediately pretended he wasn't, and Hawaiian shirt bent over to pick up something so our eyes only met for a few seconds.

That was long enough to scare me. "Charlie, come on, hurry," I said. "Let's get out of here ahead of those men. I don't want them to catch up to us."

Eddie cast a startled glance toward the men, then jerked his flight bag out from where it was wedged under the forward seat. "There's no reason why we should be afraid of them, is there?"

"If they didn't find what they wanted in Mrs. Basker's purse or her bag, maybe they think we have it," I worried. "I mean, she talked to us, and left things with us. The box of candy and her sweater. Even if we don't still have them, they may think we have whatever it is."

"They've got to be spies or crooks of some kind," Eddie said, looking as if he didn't know whether to be thrilled or terrified at the idea.

"Let's go," I said, not daring to look back along the crowded aisle, hoping the other passengers would keep the two men from moving quickly toward us. "At the time I thought it was an accident when that Upton guy kept snagging on Mrs. Basker's bag, but now I don't think so. I think he was trying to get it away from her in such a way that she wouldn't think he was stealing it, and when that didn't work, he did something more direct."

Charlie was standing waiting for us, obstructing the other passengers so that one of them said, "Excuse me, please. May I get past?"

Obediently Charlie moved to the side, speaking softly just above my ear. "They're trying to move toward us, fast. Come on."

I felt a little as if a demon were at my heels as we hurried off the plane. I didn't know what the demon could do if he caught up to us, and I didn't want to find out.

"I sure wish Aunt Molly were going to be right here," Eddie said, hitching up his shoulder strap and trotting to keep up with Charlie's long strides.

I did, too, but of course she wasn't. She was waiting for our call. "Tell me when you see a phone," I said, wondering if the men were really interested in us, really following us, and not daring to turn around to find out.

"There's one," Eddie said almost at once as we emerged into the main building and were practically swept along by the rest of the passengers.

I swung toward him, then heard Charlie say, "We can't use that one, Eddie. That's one of the white courtesy phones they have, so you can answer if they page you. We need regular pay phones. I think there may be some down that way. Come on."

It should have made me feel safer to have so many people around, but somehow it didn't.

There had been crowds in the other airport, too, but that hadn't prevented Mrs. Basker from being enticed or forced into a deserted area where she could be attacked. Having three of us didn't guarantee anything, either. Two grown men could probably handle three kids without too much trouble.

"I wonder if they've got guns," Eddie said, sounding a bit breathless. I didn't know if that was from fright or from hurrying the way we were doing.

"Thanks a lot for sharing your thoughts, Eddie," I told him. "As if I didn't have enough to worry about on my own."

"Well, if they had guns it would explain how they made Mrs. Basker go up those stairs to where nobody saw them. If they threatened to shoot her. There, there's a bunch of telephones."

I had to put down the stuff I was carrying to get out the paper with the number written on it, where we could reach Aunt Molly. By that time I had a desperate need to know if the men were following us, so I looked. To my relief, I didn't spot either a bright Hawaiian print shirt or a man in a tan one anywhere among the travelers milling around.

"Maybe I was wrong," I said hopefully, pulling the folded newspaper out of the side pocket of my flight bag. "Maybe they weren't interested in us at all. They just don't like kids, so they were giving me dirty looks."

Charlie leaned against the phone compartment, completely relaxed. "Nobody's going to try anything, anyway, in this crowd. There's a security man over there, and another pair of them down that way. If anybody scares you, yell your head off."

I laughed nervously, digging for change. "When I'm really scared—like when I have a nightmare—I try to scream, and I never can. Nothing comes out very loud."

I smoothed the paper out so I could read the number Aunt Molly had given me. The tension started to leak out of me as soon as I'd dialed it.

Only I didn't get Aunt Molly. It was her voice, but I knew immediately that it was a recording, one of those answering machines.

"Hi, this is Molly Portwood! If my caller is

Gracie, hang on, kids, I'll be there as soon as I can. My friend is having a severe asthma attack and I'm going to have to take her to the emergency room for a shot. Heaven knows how long it will take, but I hope we don't have to wait around too long. Leave a message after the beep, tell me what time you called, and I'll be there as soon as I can, okay? If I know Charlie, he's got a credit card, so why don't you kids go ahead and have dinner in the terminal, and I'll pay you back for it. Oh, and if the caller is anyone else, leave a phone number and Andrea will call you when she feels better. Bye-bye!"

Confused, almost stunned, I looked at my watch. "Uh, it's a quarter to six. Okay, Aunt Molly."

"She coming right away?" Eddie asked expectantly.

"No." I felt sort of hollow. "She's taking her friend to the emergency room. She said for us to eat dinner and charge it on Charlie's card, and she'll pay him back. She'll be here as soon as she gets her friend home from the hospital."

We stood there for a minute looking at each other. Charlie didn't seem quite so relaxed now, though he tried to be casual about glancing down the broad corridor. "Well, looks like we were running from nothing, anyway. Nobody's paying any attention to us. Shall we go find a place to eat, then, before we go down and claim our luggage? I don't think there are many places to sit down there, and we don't want to stand up for hours."

"Leave it to Aunt Molly," I said, refolding the newspaper. "Dad would say she's a real Portwood, all right. She asked me to tell her what time my call was, but she didn't tell me what time she was leaving her message. So we don't know if she left for the emergency room a couple of hours ago, or just a few minutes ago. I feel so strange, I don't know if I'm hungry or not."

"I am," Eddie stated positively. "Let's get a real meal this time. My mom's going to ask me how much junk I ate, and I'd like to be able to say truthfully that I ate salad while I was here. She doesn't have to know it was only *one* salad."

"It'll be more than one," Charlie predicted, "because Aunt Molly will see to it. I'm going to have a juicy jumbo burger with fries, and if they throw a little lettuce and tomato on the plate maybe I'll eat that, too. Let's go."

I picked up my stuff again, and although there was no sign of the men we thought had attacked Mrs. Basker, I continued to be uneasy as we went on along the concourse toward the shops. I wouldn't really feel comfortable and safe, I thought, until Aunt Molly showed up. I hoped that message had been left hours ago, so she could arrive any minute.

I stopped so suddenly that Eddie ran into me. "What if she does come soon and we're not down at the baggage place yet? She'll never find us anywhere else! This terminal is as big as Marysville, practically!"

Charlie was unfazed. "She'll have them page us, over that P.A. system, and they'll tell us to use one of the white courtesy phones. Then we'll tell her where we are, and decide where to meet. Here, how about this place? Look okay?"

Any place that got us out of the stream of people, with my back to the wall and a view of whoever was going past, sounded good to me.

We had to wait a few minutes for a table, because it was pretty crowded. There were windows along the whole side of the restaurant, so we could see everybody moving along the corridor. We had a booth on one side of a divider that ran almost the whole length of the room.

The man who waited on us was very polite. "Hi, kids. You decided what you want?"

We ordered, and by the time the food came I decided I was hungry, after all. That didn't stop me from keeping watch on the passersby, though. If Mr. Upton and Hawaiian shirt were still around, I wanted to know it.

Sometimes I thought Charlie could read minds, because he said, "They're probably gone by this time. Went down and got their luggage and grabbed an Airporter or a cab."

"They didn't have any luggage," I told him. "They didn't carry any on, anyway. Mr. Upton was about the only one I saw on the whole plane who didn't have *anything* to carry, not even a jacket or a briefcase."

Eddie's eyes suddenly grew large and he forgot to bite into the french fry he'd just dipped in ketchup; he was staring through the window.

My heart leaped painfully, and I realized I'd forgotten to watch. "What? Is it them?"

"It's sure interesting to watch people," he said. "Look at the color of that lady's hair, will you? And the jewelry and the fur coat! Why's she need a fur coat this time of year? She'll die when she gets away from the air conditioning in this place."

The lavender hair *was* unusual. I figured she had too many rings and necklaces for them to be real unless she was a movie star, and the fur coat was gorgeous, but I concentrated on getting my heart back in my chest.

"Maybe she just came from Iceland, or the Scandinavian countries," Charlie guessed. "Where it's cold. Either that or she's a movie star and wants to be noticed and doesn't care if she melts inside the coat as long as somebody knows she has it. We going to have dessert?"

We all decided on strawberry shortcake and ice cream. It wasn't quite as good as what we were used to at home, but not bad.

I began to relax, the way Charlie seemed to do so easily.

"Have you guys noticed the decor in these airports?" I asked.

"Decor?" Eddie repeated, as if he didn't know what the word meant.

"In Portland, the carpeting was a hideous mixture of red and blue, and the upholstery on the chairs was enough to make you want to close your eyes. And look at the carpet here—green and brown and orange! Who do they hire to do their decorating?"

"It's practical," Charlie said. "Doesn't show the dirt of all the thousands of feet that walk on it. Besides, don't you know the psychology of colors in restaurants and public places?"

Eddie wiped ketchup off his chin with a paper napkin. "What's psychology got to do with decorating?"

"Everything. Pale green is soothing, which is why they use it in so many hospital rooms. Certain shades of pink calm down mental patients or disturbed people who've been arrested. And colors like these"—he gestured at the floor—"are *not* restful and they make people want to hurry up and eat and leave. That way they don't linger over the tables when there are more customers waiting."

"I think it's ugly," I said. "And why do they have mirrors on the ceiling? What's the psychology of that?"

"I don't think it's psychology," Charlie decided, "but to help the waiters see what's going on behind this long divider and in the booths." He grinned. "They can spy on us."

Inadvertently, I glanced up into the mirrors. I'd only noticed them, not really looked up before.

And went cold. I mean, icy, icy cold.

There was no mistaking that shirt with the bright blue and green and scarlet print.

When my eyes got past being paralyzed, I saw something else. The top of a head going slightly bald, and I didn't recognize that, but there was also a tan shirt.

They'd pretended they didn't know each other, but they were eating together just on the other side of a thin wooden partition between our booths.

If they looked up, as I was doing now, they

could see *us*. In fact, they might even be able to *hear* us, though we certainly hadn't heard *them*.

I must have looked the way I felt, because slowly Charlie and Eddie raised their faces and stared into the overhead mirrors.

Eddie gulped and started to say something, but Charlie put a finger to his lips and shook his head.

We each had a few bites of dessert left, but nobody was hungry anymore. Charlie looked around in a calculating fashion.

To leave the restaurant, we'd have to walk past that divider, which would put us in plain view of the men I'd definitely come to consider The Enemy.

"What are we going to do?" I asked in a whisper.

Not even Charlie had an immediate answer.

# Chapter Ten

I didn't know if the awful carpeting had psychological effects on us or not, but I knew I wanted to get out of that place as fast as I could. I hadn't seen The Enemy come in—the entrance door was the one place I couldn't watch because that divider screened it from our view—but I was positive they'd come *here* because we were here already.

That meant they'd been following us, watching us, even though we hadn't seen them. And *that* meant we *really* had something to worry about.

Eddie spoke in a whisper. "I feel like a great big bird—a hawk or an eagle—is stuck in my chest, trying to get out. It . . . hurts."

"Mine, too," I whispered back.

Charlie didn't pay any attention to us. He

was looking around, and then he said in a slightly louder than normal voice, "We'll have a long ride to Aunt Molly's. Maybe we better make a pit stop before she shows up, okay? We'll get the check on the way out."

I started to remind him I'd used the rest room just before the plane landed, and then I realized that what he'd said hadn't been intended for us. It had been intended to carry to the men on the other side of that flimsy divider.

I swiveled my head around so fast it hurt. What was he talking about? What did he intend to do?

"The rest rooms are back there," he said. "Right next to the kitchen. Meet you at the cash register in a few minutes."

The rest rooms wouldn't have any outside windows to escape through, I thought. But I slid out of my chair and went with the boys, hoping Charlie had a genuine idea to get us out of here without The Enemy right on our heels. I couldn't tell to look at Charlie how *he* felt, but it was obvious Eddie was just as scared as I was.

We entered the narrow corridor opening

beneath the sign for the rest rooms, Charlie leading the way, and then I saw it.

There was a doorway opening into the kitchen from that hallway, too.

A fat man in a white apron and a little hat looked up, startled, when Charlie led the way into the kitchen.

"No admittance back here," he said. He had a big cast-iron frying pan in his hand, and it looked to me like a good way to enforce his rules if he wanted to.

"There a back door out of here? Into a different corridor than the one in from the restaurant?" Charlie asked urgently. He was carrying the bill the waiter had left with our desserts, and there were two twenty-dollar bills on top of it, all the cash he had. "Somebody's after us— not the cops or anything like that, some pretty bad dudes—and we don't want them to see us leave. You can keep the change, whatever's over the amount of the bill."

I saw suspicion in the man's face, and then he looked at the money and checked the total on the bill. It only took him a second or two to make up his mind.

"Employees entrance back there," he said, gesturing with a thumb. "All the way back, and to your left."

Charlie grinned. "Thanks. And don't tell them we came through here, okay?"

"Not unless they're security officers," the man agreed, waving us through.

I ran after Charlie, hearing Eddie behind me, past a long table where startled employees stopped making their salads and fancy-looking dishes, past a redheaded boy assembling hamburgers, letting the smells of grilling meat and onions out after us into a narrow hallway. Charlie hesitated only a moment, chose the left, and we listened to our own running feet slapping the tiled floor, heard our own gasping breaths.

When we reached a blank door at the end of the hall, Charlie shoved through it, looked in both directions, and led the way out into one of the broader passageways where a few uniformed airline employees were coming and going, paying no attention to us.

"Where are we going?" Eddie panted.

"I don't know yet," Charlie admitted. "I'm

not sure if those guys followed us into that restaurant or if it was just a coincidence, but until we *do* know, I'd rather we had a chance to work out a plan."

"A plan, yes, we need a plan," Eddie puffed. He didn't sound as if he ran as much as Charlie and I did, though we were breathing kind of heavily, too, after pelting away from those men in the restaurant. "Where do we go to do this planning?"

"Somewhere with more people than this place," I suggested strongly. "Maybe somewhere there are security guards around."

"I think they keep moving, mostly."

"Okay. Let's find one and follow along within sight of him," I said. "So if we yell he'll hear us and come to our rescue."

I couldn't help glancing back over my shoulder as we followed after a couple of flight attendants pulling their suitcases on little wheels, in case the door we had come through opened and The Enemy followed us; but by the time we came to one of the main halls there was no sign of pursuit.

We slowed our pace to a more normal one

but kept a sharp eye out in all directions. "Where the heck are we?" I asked. "I'm sure turned around."

"If we keep going this way, we should come out about where we got off the plane," Charlie said.

Eddie wasn't sure about that. "Do we want to go there? Will they look for us there?"

"I should think they might look for us down in the baggage area. Even if they don't know what luggage we had checked through, that's where the cabs and the buses come, and where anybody picking us up would probably plan to meet us."

"Then let's stay away from the baggage area." I stopped for a minute to rest my flight bag on a chair. "My arms are falling off. If we're going to run all over this terminal, maybe we ought to stick our stuff into one of those lockers and pick it up after Aunt Molly gets here. We could maybe outrun those guys if we weren't carrying so much junk."

Charlie looked thoughtfully at the bag I'd put down. "Maybe we could set a trap for them."

"Oh, sure, ambush 'em," Eddie approved.

"Surround 'em, like we're a whole posse. Hold 'em until the cops come. Only we still don't have any proof they attacked Mrs. Basker, do we?"

Charlie seemed not to hear. "Let's go back to the waiting area where we came in. There it is, right up ahead. And then we can try a couple of things. Gracie's flight bag was identical to Mrs. Basker's, wasn't it? So maybe there's a chance that's what they're after. Maybe they think whatever was supposed to be in Mrs. Basker's bag got into Gracie's by mistake."

"Nothing got into my bag by mistake," I protested.

"No, but *they* don't know that. You were talking to the old lady, and you watched her stuff for her. In fact I think there was a short time when both your bags sat side by side. Either one of you could have picked up the wrong one."

"Look and see, Gracie," Eddie said. "Maybe you *did* pick up the wrong one."

"No, I didn't. See?" I unzipped it. "There's my candy bars, and my book, and the case for my toothbrush."

"I think I'm coming up with a plan," Charlie said.

There was something about the little smile that was forming on his face that made me uneasy. "What?"

"You know how they stake out a goat in the jungle when they want the tiger to come in so they can capture it? How they use a helpless animal as bait?"

I made a choking sound. "Why are you looking at *me*?"

"Because you're the one with the blue flight bag like Mrs. Basker's. If they think maybe those bags got mixed up—"

"They can't," I interrupted. "They searched hers, remember? I think they'd know an old lady's underwear from a kid's. Besides, my book and the candy bars would give them a clue if they opened mine."

"True. But maybe they think she got confused and put whatever it is they want into *your* bag by mistake. So they want to search yours."

Indignation made me scowl. "So what are you proposing? If you think I'm going to be a sacrificial goat, Charlie, you're mistaken!

Nobody is staking me out to be slaughtered!"

"Of course not, Gracie! If I let you get kidnapped or anything like that, your dad would never let us within miles of each other again, ever. But it's got to be you, because they already know you're the one with the blue bag."

He sure wasn't making me any less apprehensive. "*What's* got to be me?"

"The bait. That's only a figure of speech; I don't expect anything to happen to you."

"What if your plan doesn't work out so *they* know they aren't supposed to make anything happen to me?" I demanded. "Forget it, Charlie! *I'm not going to act as bait!* If you don't stop talking crazy I'm going to tell Dad what you wanted me to do, and he'll probably see that you get locked up!"

"You don't even know what my plan is, yet," Charlie said, in that way he had of making everything sound reasonable even when you'd have to be a lunatic to go along with it.

"Yeah, Gracie, at least listen to his idea," Eddie said.

I glared at him. "That's easy for *you* to say. He's not talking about using *you* for bait."

"Gracie," Charlie said, kindly and with infinite patience, "nothing would happen to you. You'd be perfectly safe."

"Oh? Now that we're out of sight of those two thugs they're not dangerous anymore, is that it?"

"They're probably dangerous," Charlie conceded in a more normal voice. "But that doesn't mean they can do anything to you. Listen to my idea, anyway, will you?"

So I listened to Charlie's idea, the way I'd been doing all my life. Like the time we went up on the barn roof together, and the time we took a shortcut through Grandpa's woods and fell into the abandoned root cellar and couldn't get out until they sent a search party after us at dusk, and the time when we were just little kids when he talked me into hiding with him in an abandoned freezer and we nearly suffocated before Wayne found us and got us out.

"Gracie," Charlie asked, "are you listening?"

"I was thinking," I told him, "about the times you nearly got someone killed."

"How could I get you killed this time? In one of the busiest airports in the country, with

134

security guards all over the place? See, there's another one right now."

I had a sudden unpleasant thought. Security guards weren't quite like real cops, were they? The ones in Portland had said they'd turn the case over to the police, once they'd called for help for Mrs. Basker to be taken to the hospital. What if they didn't know what to do in a genuine emergency?

"You're not listening again. What's the matter? Don't you trust me?"

For a minute I didn't answer that. I looked full into his face, saw the curling dark red hair, the sprinkle of freckles I'd always thought so charming, the candid blue eyes, and I didn't know the answer. Did I trust Charlie? My favorite cousin, with whom I'd always had so much fun?

Charlie, who my dad thought would get somebody killed someday with his pranks?

This wasn't a prank, though. This was deadly serious, I thought, and then wished I hadn't thought *deadly*. It sounded so ominous. But we were stuck in this big airport until Aunt Molly came, and those awful men *had* hurt Mrs. Basker and tried to rob her, and they didn't deserve to get away with it.

"Okay," I said. "Tell me your plan."

Charlie is very good at explaining things. He works out details in his head very quickly. Eddie nodded a little at every one of them, but then Eddie wasn't the one who was going to be the goat.

"That's just a figure of speech," Charlie said when I expressed my uneasiness with it. "It's so simple, Gracie, and there's no more danger than just running around the way we've been doing. You understand that all you have to do is sit there and wait, don't you? Give them a chance to grab your flight bag, if that's what they want?"

"But what if they really do it? What about my toothbrush, and my other stuff that's in the bag?"

"We can take it out and store it in one of those lockers if you want to."

"But if it's empty anybody would know as soon as he picked it up."

"Okay. We can stuff something into it to give it some weight. Buy something cheap from the gift shop—"

"There isn't anything cheap in the gift shop."

"Well, look, I don't care if I lose the junk in *my* flight bag. We'll go around a corner where we're sure nobody is watching, and we'll trade what's in my bag for what's in yours. Then if they actually steal your bag, it'll be my stuff that's missing. Only it won't be missing for long, naturally, because we'll leave identification in your bag so the security men can tell they stole it when they catch them and get it back. See?"

I saw. I didn't like it a lot, but I understood. And I didn't have any better ideas. "All right," I said reluctantly. "But you guys better not really leave me alone."

"Of course not. We'll do just what I said, hide where we can watch you and call for the security guards when those guys come near you."

"I don't want to sit in *that* row of seats, though," I said, indicating the ones he'd told me would be the right place for the stakeout. "Why can't I sit with my back against the wall, like the cops do in movies, so I can see what's going on? I hate the idea of someone sneaking up behind me!"

"But that's just the point, Gracie. They *have*

to be able to sneak up behind you, or they won't try to steal your bag. Remember, put it down beside your chair, a little behind you, so it'll be easy for them to grab. And if you sense someone there, don't look around and scare them off. Let them take the bag. That'll give us evidence that they've done something wrong when we call in the security people. Then they can investigate and we'll tell them about Mrs. Basker, and maybe there will be some evidence to connect them with *that* crime that the police wouldn't even look into if we didn't catch them stealing your bag."

I didn't know if it sounded logical or not. He must have read that in my face, because Charlie added the clincher. "You don't want them to get away with what they did to Mrs. Basker, do you?"

And that's why a few minutes later I was sitting alone in a row of seats at one of the nearly deserted departure areas, my flight bag flung carelessly beside my chair, with all the little hairs prickling on the back of my neck as I waited for The Enemy to find me.

# Chapter Eleven

I knew Charlie and Eddie were posted somewhere they could see me, though just before I
took my seat I'd looked around and wasn't able
to spot them. I imagined Eddie having a hun-
ger attack and sneaking off to buy a bag of
potato chips. The boys had agreed to put their
bags into a locker, so I knew Eddie didn't have
his own food supply handy. Or maybe both of
them would go to use the bathroom, leaving
me to deal with whatever happened by myself.

I'd never felt more alone.

Maybe Dad had been right about this trip.
If either one of us had guessed what might
happen, I wouldn't be here now. I'd always
liked reading about scary adventures, but this
wasn't any fun at all.

A few people were beginning to drift into the

departure area, which had been practically empty when I sat down, and I saw by the TV screen that a flight to New York was due to leave from this gate in fifty-five minutes. At least that meant I wasn't entirely alone, but maybe that would mean The Enemy wouldn't try to steal my bag, either, if people were watching.

I wasn't sure if that made me feel better or worse. I wanted to catch those men and see them punished for what they'd done to a helpless old lady, but my skin crawled at the idea of them coming up behind me. How did I know if they'd settle for taking my bag? If they'd made Mrs. Basker go with them by threatening her with a gun, maybe they'd do the same thing to me, and then where would Charlie's plan end? What if Hawaiian shirt or Mr. Upton held me hostage in order to get away with something really valuable?

Of course I didn't have anything really valuable. Would they be so angry when they found that out that they'd shoot me? To keep me from describing them to the police who would investigate when they found my body lying like Mrs. Basker's in some deserted area, except that instead of a bruise I'd have a bullet hole in my head?

Someone walked past my chair and brushed a suitcase against my shoulder, and I nearly flew apart. "Sorry," the man said, and kept on going. He was no one I'd ever seen before. It was several minutes before my heartbeat slowed down to normal.

"Gracie, you have more imagination than is good for you," Dad said to me sometimes, and I began to think he was right. Usually I enjoyed my imagination. It was fun to make up stories and pretend to be someone I wasn't. But under the present circumstances it only made me more scared to think of things that could go wrong with Charlie's plan.

Please, Aunt Molly, I begged silently, come soon. Come and get us out of here.

But Aunt Molly didn't come. Time dragged. I decided I'd go crazy if I didn't try to find something to occupy my mind besides fantasies of being kidnapped or murdered.

I was still carrying that book I'd brought from home. I'd decided not to empty my own things out of my bag; if anything really happened, I was sure Dad or Aunt Molly would pay to replace its contents. I reached over for my bag, hoping Charlie wouldn't later say I'd spooked The Enemy just before they reached for it, and took out the book.

I couldn't read, though. On page three I realized I didn't have any idea of what I'd read, so I dropped the book back into the bag. I even repositioned the bag handles to make it easier for someone to grab it, and I took out the folded newspaper instead.

Maybe I could do the crossword puzzle. Grandma said it calmed her nerves to work on crosswords. My nerves sure needed calming.

It felt as if eyes were boring into the back of my head. I couldn't stand it and pretended to drop my pencil; I even kicked it so it rolled away from me. When I got up to retrieve it, I glanced behind me.

There was no sign of either of the men who might have been following us. There was no sign of Charlie or Eddie, either. If I ever find out they've gone away and left me alone, even for a minute, I'll kill them both, I thought grimly.

I sat down again and opened the news-paper, found the puzzle, and refolded the paper into quarters to start working on it.

Someone had already filled in some of the middle part, so I started up at the top. One across: Cracker, e.g., in five letters. I remem-bered that from one of Grandma's puzzles. W-a-f-e-r, I wrote in.

The P.A. system made an announcement, and I realized I hadn't been paying attention when they came to the part about using one of the white courtesy telephones. My heart leaped. Aunt Molly? Had they said Molly?

The message was repeated. "Will Dennis Malloy go to the nearest white courtesy tele-phone, please."

Deflated, I slumped in my seat. If Aunt Molly had any idea what we were going through, I thought, she'd leave her friend in the hands of the doctors and call the police to meet her here at the airport, sirens screaming.

Except, of course, that The Enemy hadn't done anything since we left Portland to be arrested for. So far.

I tried to go back to the puzzle. Twenty-two

across: Stanley Gardner, in four letters. I knew that one, because my dad's a Perry Mason fan, and I read the books sometimes, too. I wrote in E-a-r-l, then erased it and changed it to E-r-l-e.

That meant, I thought, trying to concentrate, that eighteen down, German for mister in four letters, was h-e-r-r.

The next one had me stymied: mispickle, in three letters. Mispickle? What the heck was that? It sounded like somebody made a mistake making a pickle, but I never heard of anything like that.

I decided to skip that one and pick something that tied into the words Hawaiian shirt had already written in. Hirsute, in five letters. Wasn't that h-a-i-r-y? Only it didn't fit, because where I needed an "r" there was an "x."

I stared at the word the original owner of the paper had penciled in. It was supposed to be "obliterate," which I was pretty sure meant "erase," but what Hawaiian shirt had written in didn't make any sense. It was a jumble of meaningless letters and numbers. I never saw numbers in a crossword puzzle before, not unless they were written out.

I supposed I could erase—obliterate—the wrong things that were written in. I turned the pencil upside down and scrubbed out a couple of the numbers, and then felt a surge of fear as I both saw and heard my blue flight bag go skittering across the floor, away from me.

Charlie had told me not to look around if I thought The Enemy was stealing my bag, because the idea was to let him get away with it, but I couldn't help it.

I turned my head in time to see a young man in jeans, athletic shoes, and a yellow T-shirt with blue letters that said GO SEA HAWKS on it picking up the bag and bringing it back to me. "Sorry," he said, and dropped it beside my chair before he hurried away.

With that shirt he had to be from Seattle, I figured. Which could mean he was connected with The Enemy, who had come from there. But he didn't seem to be trying to steal anything. His Nikes were about size thirteens, and the bag was sticking out too far; he just caught his foot in the straps and kicked it before he could stop.

I repositioned the bag, my chest hurting

145

from the tension. Darn Charlie and his stupid ideas, anyway! I gave up the idea of trying to do a stupid puzzle that someone else had already spoiled. I decided I'd better keep the telephone number Aunt Molly had given me, in case I had to call it again, so I tore off the edge of the newspaper and stuck the scrap with the writing on it in the pocket of my jeans. Then I refolded the newspaper and stuck it back in the outside pocket of the flight bag.

How long was I supposed to sit here like this, with nothing happening except that I was scared out of my wits? I looked around, hoping to spot Charlie and tell him I'd had it, that his plan wasn't working and he'd have to think of something else.

And then something *did* happen.

I saw him coming across the expanse of polished tile, straight at me.

The man in the Hawaiian shirt.

I sucked in a sharp breath, frantically searching for Charlie. Where was he? How far away had he and Eddie gone to make themselves inconspicuous?

Then I spotted Eddie, sitting on the floor

quite a way down the building near another boarding area, his back against a pillar. He was facing straight this way, but the trouble was he didn't see either me or The Enemy, because he was reading a comic book and he didn't look up.

I'd have been angry but I was too scared. There was no doubt about it, the man I was afraid of was coming right to me, and there was no sign of Charlie or any of the security men.

I gulped and tried to think what to do. If I screamed, would the people around me come to my rescue? Or would they pretend it had nothing to do with them and ignore it, even if The Enemy started to drag me away?

I didn't even know if I *could* scream. My mouth felt the way it had the time I was being initiated into one of Charlie's clubs, when I'd been blindfolded and told I was going to have to swallow cod liver oil. I hated cod liver oil, and I braced myself for it and vowed I'd get even later. Instead they'd stuck a spoonful of feathers in my mouth. For a minute I thought I'd choke on them, or suffocate, before I got them all off my tongue.

The Enemy had arrived. He came right up to me, but he didn't try to take my bag. His face was ugly, and he was angry. "I think you took something of mine," he said to my astonishment. "You stole my newspaper."

My jaw dropped open. My scream faded into a whimper. Where was Charlie? What was I supposed to do now?

I tried to speak and at first all I could do was squeak. "I—I thought you were through with it!" I finally managed.

"Well, I wasn't. So I'd like it back." He didn't wait for me to reply; he simply bent over and pulled the folded paper out of the pocket of my flight bag and slapped it against his thigh. For a minute I thought maybe he was going to slap *me* with it.

"Next time," he said in a menacing manner, "keep your hands off other people's belongings."

"B-but I thought you'd thrown it away, I d-didn't know you were coming b-back—" I hadn't stuttered since I had speech therapy in the second grade. It didn't matter. He wasn't listening, anyway. He turned around and walked away, leaving me dazed.

He hadn't struck me. He hadn't threatened me with a gun. He hadn't even stolen my flight bag.

Was it all over now? Was this all that was going to happen?

I was shaking. And angry. I still didn't see Charlie, but when I turned Eddie was there.

He was staring at me with his mouth open.

"What happened?" he demanded.

"What did it look like?" I asked, sounding waspy. "He said I stole his paper and he wanted it back, so he took it. What were *you* doing when he came up to me? He could have—have stabbed me or anything!"

"He didn't have a knife," Eddie protested. "He didn't hurt you."

"But he could have! Fat lot of good you and Charlie were!" I cried, feeling near tears I struggled to control. As upset as I was, I knew I'd never live it down if I bawled about it.

And then I saw Charlie coming. I guessed he'd been crouched behind a divider at one of the adjoining boarding gates, and he didn't seem in the least perturbed. "You okay, Gracie? What did he say to you?"

I was trying to calm down. "Where were you? Why didn't you come to my rescue, the way you were supposed to?"

Charlie fell into his reasonable voice. "He didn't touch you. Didn't take anything except the newspaper that really was his, after all. I couldn't call a security officer for that. And what good would it have done for me to walk out and confront him? I couldn't very well demand that he let you keep the paper, could I?"

"You could have given me a little m-moral support!" I blurted. "I was scared to death!"

"You did great, Gracie. Didn't she, Eddie? Only we didn't get any evidence that he's done anything wrong." That seemed to be his main concern.

"I don't care about him anymore. Let's try calling Aunt Molly again, see if she's at her friend's or has gone home or what. I wish I knew which hospital she took her friend to and I'd call her there. I want to get out of here!"

"Yeah, okay, maybe you're right. Let's go back to the phones," Charlie said, giving in.

"Why did he want the newspaper?" Eddie wondered as we walked toward the bank of telephones. "I mean, did he fly all the way here from Seattle just to get back a newspaper? He could have bought another paper there a lot cheaper."

Charlie stopped walking to look at him with admiration. "Eddie, that's a good thought. I mean, I'm sure he had a better reason for flying to San Francisco, but what was so important about the paper? And if he saw you picking it up, Gracie, why didn't he say something at the time?"

"He wasn't anywhere around when I picked it up," I said. "I looked for him, to be sure."

"How'd he know you were the one who had it, then?" Charlie chewed speculatively on his lower lip. "If he didn't see you pick it up?"

"She had the top of the paper with the name on it, *Seattle Times,* sticking over the edge of the pocket on the bag," Eddie offered.

"Sure, but plenty of people on Flight 211 had newspapers, and probably most of them were copies of the *Seattle Times.* And if all he wanted was the news, he could have bought a copy of the *San Francisco Chronicle* right there." He gestured at a vending rack of papers.

"Who knows?" I dug into my pocket for the scrap of paper that had the telephone number on it. "Maybe he wanted to finish his crossword puzzle. Though he's sure not very good at them."

And that was when it hit me.

The boys said afterward that I went so pale they thought I was going to faint.

"What?" Charlie asked when I sagged against the side of the phone cubicle. "What's the matter? Are you sick?"

"Maybe," I said weakly. "I mean—I think I know why he wanted the paper back. Sort of. It *was* because of the crossword puzzle."

"Oh, come on," Charlie began, but I waved him into silence.

"He'd done part of the puzzle," I said. "Only he didn't put in the right letters for the words it called for. I didn't notice what he'd filled in until I tried to do some of the other spaces and they didn't match up with what he'd written. Some of his fill-ins weren't even letters; they were mostly numbers."

There was noise and movement around us, but it was as if we were in a cocoon of our own, a bubble that shut out everything but the three of us.

"He left the paper on his seat on purpose," Charlie said slowly, "for somebody else to pick up. Because there was a message in it. In the crossword puzzle."

And then we all three spoke together; even Eddie figured it out.

"In code," we said. "A message in code!"

# Chapter Twelve

Eddie repeated the words, sounding dazed. "A message in code. Geez! What did it say, Gracie?"

I remembered how he'd sat there reading his stupid old comic book instead of watching what was happening to me. It made my tone sarcastic. "It was *in code,* Eddie. That means it wasn't written in plain English. I *don't know what it said!*"

"No, I mean, what were the letters written out? Maybe we can decipher the code. Can you remember what the letters were?"

"He's right," Charlie said. "If you remember them, write them down right away before you forget what they were."

"You guys are still getting secret messages out of cereal boxes. This one isn't going to say the treasure is hidden behind the couch, or whatever. This is something serious."

"Sure. We know that. Here." Charlie reached over and took the scrap of newspaper out of my hand, turning it over so he didn't write on top of the phone number Aunt Molly had given me. "You talk, and I'll write. Let's get it down. You *do* remember it, don't you? It wasn't very long, was it?"

"No, but I'm not sure I can remember it all. I didn't realize it was important," I said, but I recited what I thought the letters and numbers had been, and Charlie carefully wrote them out and looked at them.

"*X's*. And more numbers than letters. Hmmm."

I had an unpleasant thought. "I was trying to fit in *my* words, and I erased a couple of his letters. They may be mad when they find out it's not all still there." And come looking for me? I wondered, to ask what I'd erased? I'd thought it was all over when The Enemy walked away with the newspaper, and now it occurred to me that it might *not* be over, that they might shoot me if I didn't tell them what I'd erased. I swallowed audibly.

"The newspaper belonged to the guy in the

loud shirt," Eddie pointed out. "He must know what he wrote there."

"Then why is he here? Why did he come up and take it away from me?"

"Yeah," Charlie said, not making me feel any better. "If he wrote it there himself, and—say—left it on his seat for someone else to pick up—like Mr. Upton—only Mr. Upton saw *Gracie* take the paper. And the Upton guy knew he'd lost it so he quick went and called Hawaiian shirt, wherever he'd gone, so he'd know. That's why he was late getting on the plane. Told them at the desk it was an emergency or something." He paused to think, working it out in his head. "Let's see. Upton knew somehow that Gracie gave the paper to Mrs. Basker. He saw her stick it in her flight bag—the old lady, I mean—and after he got on the plane he tried to get the bag away from her long enough to get the paper back. He apparently *didn't* see her give the paper to Gracie, and when his attempts to steal the bag didn't work—remember how he tried to get the seat next to Mrs. Basker? And how grouchy he was when the flight attendant said he had to sit where he'd been assigned?—he used some ruse to get her off where he could hit her over the head and search her stuff."

"He probably pulled a gun on her," Eddie said, nodding. "Told her he'd shoot her if she didn't go with him."

"Sure. And when he didn't find the paper, he figured she must have passed it along to Gracie, who kept talking to her, so they started watching *us*. And when they realized Gracie actually had the paper, the guy in the loud shirt just walked up to her and took it."

It sounded horribly logical, but there were a lot of gaps. "But if the guy in the Hawaiian shirt *wrote* the message, why would he need the paper back? Why would he fly all the way to Portland to get it, when he apparently hadn't intended to get on our plane in the first place?"

"He didn't remember what it was," Eddie said promptly. "That's why people write things down, like you wrote down the telephone number for Aunt Molly's friend. It's hard to remember numbers. Especially if you're middle-aged, Mom says."

"Or maybe he was only a messenger," Charlie contributed. "Maybe he didn't *write* the message, he was just supposed to *deliver* it to someone at the airport—Upton—who would then carry it away to San Francisco."

"So why did the other man follow him, then?"

"Follow *us*, I think. I'll bet Upton wasn't sure he'd recognize us, especially Mrs. Basker. So he wanted Hawaiian shirt along to be sure he got the right person. And the message is important; they couldn't take a chance on losing it."

"Yeah," Eddie chimed in. "I'll bet the guy in the Hawaiian shirt even chartered a plane to catch up with us in Portland, to make sure they got the code message back."

"Only we weren't supposed to land in Portland," I objected, "so how would he know he could—uh-oh."

I didn't like the idea that had just struck me. It struck Charlie at just about the same time.

"Maybe," Charlie said, almost whispering, "he *made* us land in Portland, to give him time to catch up with us. Maybe he called the airlines and told them there was a bomb on Flight 211. They wouldn't take any chances with a planeload of passengers and crew. They'd come down as soon as they could, and call out the people who look for bombs."

Eddie liked that idea, which was more than I did. It made me sure that none of this was a joke, none of it was harmless, and that when the men realized they didn't have the entire message they would be back—after *me*.

"How could he know it would be Portland where we'd land, though?" I asked, hoping my speculations were crazy.

"We were on a 727. It's too big to land at any of the little airports anywhere else. Portland International was the only logical place, short of San Francisco," Charlie asserted.

"There wasn't any bomb," Eddie said, sounding awed. "They just wanted to get their newspaper back, with the message in it. Wow! It must be something really important!"

"And crooked," Charlie added. "Very crooked."

"And dangerous," I croaked. "Dangerous for us."

After a moment of silence, Charlie handed me the scrap of the edge of the newspaper we'd written on. "Here. Try calling Aunt Molly again."

My finger was unsteady as I dialed; I held my breath, willing her to answer in person.

"Hi, this is Molly Portwood! If my caller is Gracie, hang on, kids, I'll be there as soon as I can—"

I must have looked as bleak as I sounded. "It's the same recorded message. She's not back yet."

Eddie was less excited and more anxious than he'd been a minute ago. "Maybe we ought to call home and tell them what's going on," he said uncertainly.

"What good would that do?" Charlie asked before I could voice my opinion. "It must be eight hundred miles or more and a couple of hours away even if they flew down here. A day and a half if they drive. They could murder all three of us before our folks could get here, if they wanted to."

"So what are we going to do? We're sitting ducks," I said. "Even in this great big airport, surrounded by people, we're sitting ducks. Charlie, we'd better go to the police. Talk to the security guards and ask them to lock us up— in protective custody, sort of"—I watched TV shows, too—"until Aunt Molly shows up, or else have them call the regular police."

"We could do that," Charlie said, but he sounded as if he were thinking again, and I knew that going into protective custody wasn't what he wanted to do. "On the other hand—"

"I don't think I want to know what you think on the other hand," I said, and I wasn't kidding.

As usual, he didn't pay any attention to what he didn't want to consider. "If we do that, chances are it will be hours—if ever—before we get anyone to believe us. To believe that bomb threat was to slow us down so these mysterious guys could catch up with us. To investigate this situation."

I started to shake my head. "No, Charlie. No, it's not up to *us* to investigate it. We're just kids, and we don't know anything about—"

He interrupted me. "We know it's real. We know we're not making it up because we watched one too many cop shows on TV. And we have the coded message—most of it, anyway, if Gracie remembered it accurately. Maybe we can figure it out. Maybe we can turn the tables—find those guys and watch *them* and see what they do. Make sure they don't get away with their crooked business, whatever it is."

The first time I ever went swimming in the ocean and got knocked down by a big wave, I felt sort of like I felt then. Cold and numb and terrified.

That time in the ocean my dad had been there to grab my hand and pull me out.

Now there were only Charlie and Eddie, and I was beginning to think maybe Dad was right about Charlie: Maybe he did attract disasters the way movie stars drew photographers. He didn't usually get hurt—not too much, anyway—but what if this time he wasn't so lucky? What if none of us were lucky?

In the middle of those hundreds of people traveling—maybe there were thousands of them right there in that one airport—I felt as alone as I'd ever been in my whole life. Dad was at least four hours away from me. Even if he could get an immediate flight it would take him almost that long to actually get here, by the time he arranged for reservations and drove to Sea-Tac from where we lived in Marysville.

I couldn't depend on my dad to save me this time.

Charlie was watching my face, reading my emotions. "Eddie and I could keep on investigating, and let you go into protective custody, I guess," he said.

He sounded neutral, as if it didn't matter whether I stayed with the boys or not, but I had a sudden picture of going back home and having everyone know I'd been a baby, that I'd chickened out before they did. (At least you'd be a *live* chicken, a tiny voice said in the back of my brain.)

My voice shook a little. "I don't suppose they could actually do anything to us in such a public place, if we stick together. At least, they wouldn't actually shoot where people would see them."

"They wouldn't shoot you, anyhow," Eddie

volunteered, "not until you told them what they want to know, about what you erased from their message."

"If that's supposed to be comforting," I told him, my heart thudding, "you might as well know it isn't working."

I had been standing there with the receiver to my ear, hearing all of Aunt Molly's recorded message, and when it came to an end I'd hung up. I didn't know what else to do. It seemed pointless to try to explain to the answering machine what was happening to us. She might panic and try to get to us so fast she'd wreck her car or something.

"Eddie's right. They didn't kill Mrs. Basker. There's no reason to think they'd murder us, either. What good would that do them?" Charlie and his logic again.

"She's an old lady, and she really didn't know what they were talking about. They knocked her out. That *could* have killed her."

Charlie straightened up, throwing his shoulders back, and I knew he'd made up his mind what *he* was going to do.

"You want us to take you to the security

guards and leave you to explain what's going on, see what they do?"

I met his gaze bleakly. I was pretty sure I knew what they'd do. They wouldn't listen, not seriously, and if they locked me up, it wouldn't necessarily be in protective custody. I wondered if they had mental wards at Juvenile Hall.

"Or do you want to stay with Eddie and me?" Charlie asked.

My throat hurt so it was hard to speak. "I guess I'll stay with you. Only don't do anything really stupid and get us hurt, okay?"

Charlie grinned. "Trust me," he said.

# Chapter Thirteen

"What we need," Eddie proposed when we huddled together to plan our strategy, "is disguises. I mean, it's going to be hard to stalk those guys—if we can find them again—without being noticed. Since they obviously followed us and know what we look like."

"Great idea," Charlie told him. "Let's go back to the gift shop and get some inconspicuous stuff, T-shirts, something different from what they've seen us in. Everybody's wearing jeans, so those won't matter."

"Not inconspicuous," Eddie contradicted. "We'll still be three middle-sized kids, and we're not particularly conspicuous now. What we need is to look so different that they won't pay any attention unless they get a good look at our faces. I mean *real* different.

Come on, I'll show you what I had in mind."

We picked out a fluorescent lime green shirt for me with a picture of cable cars on it, and sunglasses with multicolor striped frames, and a bright yellow straw hat with a purple ribbon and a floppy brim. I'd look different, all right.

Eddie chose a San Francisco Giants T-shirt and a baseball cap, and Charlie selected a shirt with purple and white flowers all over it. Then he studied a pair of plaid walking shorts. "I wonder if my dad will have a fit over what I'm charging? These would sure look different from what I have on."

Eddie grinned. "Think of it as an investment in our futures—like staying alive, right? Your dad would approve of *that,* I think. Go ahead, get the shorts. It makes a great outfit. If those guys look at your clothes they'll go blind and won't be able to see your face."

"They'll still see his hair," I pointed out. Not many people had that kind of red curly hair. "And your hair shows through the top of that visor cap you've got on, so one of those won't help."

"Wait a minute. I think I saw some visor

caps that aren't open on the top," Eddie said, darting off into a side aisle. "Yeah, here, how about this one?"

It was orange, and it looked horrible with the shirt and the shorts, but it did cover Charlie's hair. I had to close my eyes, thinking about it, and he didn't even have the new clothes on yet.

"As many weirdos as there are walking around this place," Eddie observed, his gaze following a couple of girls with spiky hairdos, one in pink and the other in blue and green (my mom once threatened to shave my head if I ever turned up looking like that), "nobody will notice us at all in these outfits."

The total price, when the clerk filled out the slip for the credit card purchase, was high enough to make me wince. I hoped Uncle Jim would be understanding about it when the bill came in. The clerk must have been used to strange purchases, because she didn't comment on them.

"We'll change in the rest rooms," Charlie said, taking charge at once as we left the gift shop, "and put our other clothes and Gracie's flight bag into one of those lockers, so we won't have anything to carry that might be recognized."

We looked different, all right, when we regrouped ten minutes later. "The trouble is," I said, "we're still three kids—two boys and a girl—and that's going to make us suspect right there, isn't it?"

For once I'd thought of something that hadn't occurred to Charlie. "Yeah," he said thoughtfully. "Maybe we better split up."

Alarmed, I said, "Don't dump me off by myself again, not if you're going to keep track of me the way you did the last time. That guy could have killed me and escaped before either one of you even yelled for a security patrol."

"Gosh, Gracie, you keep having these gruesome ideas," Charlie chided, as if I were a little kid. "I'm surprised at the kind of TV your folks must let you watch."

I sounded grim. "It's the kind of thing you see on the news all the time. Gruesome things happen, every day, to perfectly ordinary people."

He didn't argue with that. "I'll hang behind,

then, and keep my eye out. You and Eddie go together, and we'll look for The Enemy." The boys had picked up my phrase for Mr. Upton and the guy in the Hawaiian shirt. "But first let's get rid of this stuff. We can put our bags in one of those lockers over there, but it won't hold all of this, too, so we'll have to rent another one. Anybody got any more change? I've only got a quarter."

Our plan was, first, to find The Enemy. Then we were to watch them, follow them if necessary, and see where they went and what they did.

So we stowed our stuff and started strolling along the concourse, Eddie and I ahead, Charlie some distance behind on the other side, all of us checking the business places to see if we could spot The Enemy.

The P.A. system made an announcement every few minutes. It wasn't always easy to understand, and I hoped that if Aunt Molly called for us we'd hear it. What I most fervently hoped, as a matter of fact, was that I'd hear her paging us before we found The Enemy. She'd know what to do when we told her what was going on, and unlike the police, she'd probably believe us.

We went all the way out to where we'd have to pass out of one of the security checkpoints without seeing either of the men, and turned around to make another pass along the concourse. As we passed a bank of vending machines a man in a gray suit was buying a paper; he pocketed his change and folded the paper, turning just before we reached him, and met my eyes for just a second.

Something twitched inside me in sudden consternation. Eddie seemed to know, though I hadn't made any sound; he stooped to retie his shoelace, speaking out of the corner of his mouth in a hoarse whisper. "What's the matter? You see 'em?"

"No." I walked on a few steps before I paused and waited for him to catch up. "No, but I think maybe they've called in reinforcements."

I had to reach out and grab his arm to keep him from turning around.

"Yeah? Who? Where?"

"The way that man looked at me. As if he

171

*knew* me, only I never saw him before. The one in the gray suit. Don't be obvious about looking at him, okay?"

When we both turned, ever so casually, the man was consulting his watch and didn't appear to be paying any attention to us at all. But I knew. He was quite aware of us, and it made my throat tighten up so it was difficult to speak. "Can't you feel it? Like—like cold air coming from him!"

Eddie licked his lips. "No. Maybe he gave you a funny look because he doesn't like kids. Or he thinks your outfit is freaky. Something like that. Come on, let's test it."

"How?" I asked stupidly. All I could think of was that we were surrounded by enemies, and Aunt Molly still hadn't come to rescue us.

"Let's go in that restaurant. Pretend we're going to eat. See what he does. Look, we can go in that door and wait a minute, then come out the other one over there."

I caught a glimpse of Charlie, pretending to be reading something in a window a hundred yards away. Did he notice where we were going? I wondered, heart fluttering.

There were plenty of people in the restaurant, but that didn't make me feel any better. A gangster wouldn't worry about crowds; he'd do whatever he wanted to do. At least that was the way it was in the movies.

The man in the gray suit didn't follow us inside. But when we came out the other door a few minutes later and headed rapidly away from him, he began to stroll after us. I saw him reflected in a window, and put down an urge to run.

Eddie was chewing on his lower lip. "Geez, maybe you're right. He *does* seem to be following us. Let's be absolutely sure. Let's do an abrupt turnaround and walk the other way. If he's not interested in us he won't pay any attention. People are doing crazier things than that on every side of us."

Of course it would look suspicious if the man had any reason to be suspicious, but I didn't have any better idea. When Eddie said loudly, "I must have dropped that five-dollar bill! Let's go back and see if it's on the floor in that restaurant!" and swung around, I went with him.

We took the man in the gray suit by surprise. He was looking right at us, and though his gaze immediately went through us, past us, neither Eddie nor I had any doubt. He *was* watching us. We didn't look to see if he turned, so we didn't know until we got back to where Charlie was looking at an exhibit of Indian artifacts that the man had stopped and was again checking the time and pretending *not* to be watching us.

"What's going on?" Charlie hissed, not getting too close to us when we paused. "Who's *that* guy?"

"He *is* following us," I said. "Isn't he?"

"Looks like it to me. Who the heck is he?"

"We don't know. He looked right at me, Charlie, and I'm *scared*! It was like he could see *through* me! Those other guys must have called him in to help—"

"How did he know who we were? They couldn't have described us in our disguises, and we split up so we wouldn't be a trio . . ."

I had a dismal, hollow feeling. "I don't know. I hoped when they got the newspaper back they'd leave us alone, only if none of them

174

know what's missing where I erased a few letters—" I drew in a deep breath. "What if they try to force me to tell them what's missing, and I don't remember it right?"

It was easy to recall what had happened to Mrs. Basker and think what it would be like to have it happen to *me*.

"Maybe you better look at it again, see if it sounds right, the way we put it down." He pulled the little slip of paper out of his pocket. I was surprised that he had it with him, since we'd changed clothes.

"What good will that do?" I asked bitterly. "I told you what I thought it had said. I'm not likely to remember any better now than I did then. And if all this disguise business is for nothing—"

I didn't finish that sentence. Eddie said what I was thinking as he shoved his glasses back up onto the bridge of his nose. "We're doomed," he said in a stage whisper.

Charlie gave us a disgusted glare. "No, we're not! Come on, if we've blown our cover, let's go sit down and have a cold drink. This stuff is making me thirsty. Gracie can look at this again and see if she remembers anything else. Naturally, if they try to force you to tell them what you know, you'll tell them. Whatever they're involved in, it's not worth getting killed or even hurt over. Come on, we can get Cokes over there."

We pooled our cash to pay for the drinks, which didn't taste as good as the Cokes I was used to at home. Maybe that was only because I was so scared that anything would have tasted like poison. When Charlie spread out the torn scrap of newspaper on the table in front of us, I didn't even look at it.

Because the man in the gray suit had just walked up to the counter and ordered a cup of coffee. He stood there drinking it, not looking directly at us, but in a position where he couldn't possibly miss it when we left. It hurt for me to breathe.

Charlie jiggled the paper. "Come on, Gracie, I see him, too, but he's not doing anything, and there are two security officers taking a break right over there. The guy isn't going to do anything. Look at this. Try to remember if there was anything else. Maybe the easiest thing would be to walk up to him and give him this and tell him that's all you remember of what was on the puzzle."

I choked and grabbed for a napkin to keep from spraying Coke all over the table. Eddie patted my arm encouragingly. "You okay now? Go ahead, look at it. Maybe Charlie's got a good idea."

"The ideas he's had so far haven't exactly been terrific," I said, but I smoothed out the scrap of newspaper. "This is upside down," I told them, "that's the number Aunt Molly gave me. Where *is* she?"

With exaggerated patience, Charlie reached out to turn the paper over. "Here, then, read this side."

I scowled at it. It didn't mean any more to me now than it had earlier. And then something clicked.

"What is it? You remembered what you erased?" Charlie leaned toward me, his elbows on the table.

I picked up the paper, looked at what I'd dictated for him to write there, then reversed the scrap and looked at the number where

I'd called Aunt Molly. And then I turned it right side up again and took my fingers away from it.

"You . . ." I hesitated, not wanting to sound like an idiot if I was wrong. "You know what this looks like? I mean, if you take out the letters that don't seem to mean anything, what do the numbers look like to you?"

The boys twisted their heads to read it better.

"Nothing," Eddie said.

"Just random numbers," Charlie said, shrugging.

I inhaled deeply and tried to pretend that the hostile man in the gray suit wasn't drinking coffee only a few yards away. "It looks like a telephone number."

Charlie was first startled, then excited. "You're right! It does! The pattern is the same—three numbers, and an *X*—that's for the dash—and then four numbers, and then it's an *L*." Now he was frowning. "The whole string of numbers is preceded by a *P*—for phone, maybe? The *X* could be just a spacer, and then . . ." His voice trailed off. "I don't know what the numbers are after the *L*. Four digits. Not another phone number."

My mind was blank—well, almost blank. I was still scared—but Eddie's wasn't. "L for locker," he said in a low voice. "And there are four-digit numbers on those lockers where we put our stuff, remember?" Charlie cleared his throat. "Let's go call Aunt Molly again," he said, and stood up, forgetting the drink he'd said he needed to quench his thirst.

It wasn't until we'd left the restaurant (with the man in the gray suit casually following a moment later) that Charlie added under his breath, "Let's find out if those numbers match up with any of the pay phones here in the airport. And then we'll check out the locker numbers." He grinned at us. "If it *is* a locker number here in the airport, it could be a phone number here, too, couldn't it? I think maybe we're finally getting somewhere."

I trotted along between the boys, and I sure hoped he was right.

# Chapter Fourteen

The man in the gray suit had disappeared. We didn't see the two we had dubbed The Enemy, either. But I didn't feel any safer. Maybe they were in disguises, too. Or maybe they'd called in even more reinforcements, so that any of the people we saw might be enemies.

There was an old woman in a dirty coat— even though it was summer—with all kinds of junk in a shopping bag, who watched us with interest when we checked on the numbers in the first bank of phones. I even suspected *her,* but when we moved on, she didn't follow us.

And there was a young guy with long stringy hair, in patched jeans and a sweatshirt so faded I couldn't even guess what color it had originally been. He lounged against a wall, smoking a cigarette, and kept an eye on us too.

When I murmured something to call the boys' attention to him, Charlie dismissed him with a glance.

"He's just bumming around, killing time until somebody comes in on a plane, probably. Nobody to worry about."

"But he's watching us," I hissed.

"It's probably our outfits," Eddie volunteered. "You know, the same as we watched the lady with the purple hair and all the jewelry."

"It's none of these numbers," Charlie said a minute later, after checking half a dozen pay phones.

"It wouldn't have to be any of the telephones in the airport," I said glumly as we moved along toward the next bank of telephones, which were all over the place. "It could be phones anywhere in San Francisco."

"But it looks like locker numbers, too," Eddie said. "Which sort of suggests a place where there are both lockers and pay phones, don't you think? Like a bus station or an airport, and since the guy with the coded message was flying in here, the airport's more likely. We better do this systematically, or we're going to forget which phones we've already checked."

"Right. Straight down this side, back up the other side, then we do the same in all the other concourses, and on the other levels."

"We could be here for weeks," I said, discouraged. "And we may be wrong about it being a phone number in the first place."

"Well, until Aunt Molly comes, or The Enemy show up and kidnap us," Charlie said, annoyingly cheerful, "we've got nothing else to do, anyway. So let's check phone numbers."

"And when we go past a bank of lockers," Eddie added, "we'll check those, too."

We found the locker number first. I stared at it, disbelieving. Four-seven-eight-two. I moistened my lips and rechecked it against the scrap of paper. I squeaked when I touched Charlie's arm to get his attention.

"This is it! This is the right locker! Isn't it?"

Charlie read the numbers aloud. "Four-seven-eight-two! Hey, it is!"

We stared at the locker as if by sheer willpower we might be able to see what was inside it. "What do you suppose it is? Microfilm?

Stolen jewels? Stolen military secrets?" Eddie was half-grinning, half-scared. "Or maybe drugs?"

I glanced quickly around, but I didn't see anyone at the moment who appeared to be observing us, though that didn't give me any sense of security.

"What do we do now?"

"We keep looking for the phone number," Charlie said promptly. "If we were right about the lockers, we could very well be right about the phone number. Come on, let's hit the next bank of phones down there."

"There are so many we could easily miss some," I commented as we reluctantly left the locker area.

"Sure. I know there are a whole lot more phones downstairs, near the baggage area and the rental car booths. But I'm making a bet," Charlie said, "that it will be somewhere near that locker. Because it doesn't make sense, does it, that whoever's supposed to get the message from the newspaper is going to have to run all over the whole airport to do whatever he has to do with the phone and the locker."

"Put something in, or take something out,"
Eddie said.

And once again Charlie was right.

In a secluded section of phones, some of
the most private ones we'd found, there were
the numbers we were looking for. I didn't
remember what the final digit had been, but
the first numbers were the same as the ones
we had written down from the crossword
puzzle. And the adjoining phones had con-
secutive numbers, all beginning like the number we had, with the final digit different in
each booth.

I practically tingled with excitement, and I
could see that the boys did, too. Only I didn't
know what was supposed to happen next.
"What do we do now? Wait here until someone
calls one of these phones? It's probably too
late, the call has already been made. That
would explain why we haven't seen any more
of The Enemy. They got what they wanted, and
they left the airport." I felt relieved, yet disappointed, too.

Charlie looked thoughtfully around the
open cubicles. "I don't think so. Unless you

forgot part of that message written into the puzzle, it didn't give a time or a date or anything like that. A person wouldn't know when to expect a call. And nobody would just sit here for hours, or days, waiting for one. No, it has to be something else."

"Something connected with the locker," I said slowly. The only thing I could think of that would connect with the locker was . . . "A key," I thought aloud. "They'd need a key to get into the locker, wouldn't they? But how would that be connected to a phone number?"

"Maybe," Charlie said, running a hand over the top of the divider between one cubicle and the next, "it's not the *number* that's important, but the *booth*. Maybe this is where they left another message . . . or the key."

"I can't remember what that last number was!" I cried in frustration, then remembered to lower my voice, although we were sort of off the main traffic area, and there was hardly anybody close to us. "So how do we know which booth? And what good will it do us if we figure it out? Charlie, what if it's the key—or a message—and they've taped it somewhere in one of the booths? What if the number of the phone is just to tell which booth to look in?"

It was in the third one we tried. I put my hand under the little shelf that gave you a place to write or rest a purse. There was old used chewing gum under there, and I almost jerked my hand away, and then I felt it.

Hard metal, small, key-shaped, and covered with Scotch tape.

"Bingo!" I said, and pulled it free.

I held it out on my palm, and Charlie nodded, grinning from ear to ear.

"Let's see if it fits the locker. Anybody want to bet that it doesn't?"

"No takers," Eddie assured him, grinning, too. "It's got the number right on it, see?"

"Why did they need the number in the coded message if it was on the key?" I wondered.

"Insurance, maybe," Charlie guessed. "Double checking, sort of. Or to make it possible for whoever was picking up whatever's in the locker to locate the right locker first, before he had the key on him. It would be faster that way, for a getaway. This has to be something illegal, so they'd want to pick up the merchandise, whatever it is, and take off as soon as possible."

We had to force ourselves not to run back to the lockers. I even forgot to watch for The Enemy, I was so excited. What would we find?

My fingers were unsteady as I inserted the little key into the lock.

The door swung open, and we stared into the locker at a briefcase, one of those thick metal ones. For the first time it occurred to me that we might be doing something illegal ourselves to touch it.

I hesitated. "What if what they're doing *isn't* against the law? What if we're interfering in a legitimate business? People must use these lockers for such things—"

"Sure. They're the good guys, right?" Charlie said. "They knocked an old lady over the head and stole her stuff, put her in the hospital. Come on, let's take it out and see if we can get into it."

I just stood there, looking at the briefcase, which had to be very important—and not ours—until Charlie made a sound of disgust and shoved me aside.

"Okay. I've got it. Now let's go somewhere private and see if we can find out what it is."

"What about the key?" Eddie asked, hesitating. "Do you think maybe we should lock the locker again and stick the key back where it was? I mean, it looks like they didn't get all the message because they didn't know the part Gracie remembered, so they didn't find the phone yet, or they'd have taken the key. Should we put it back where we found it?"

"We don't have any tape or anything—" Charlie began, but I interrupted.

"We've got chewing gum! We'll stick it on with that!"

So that's what we did. By now I was so nervous I had goose bumps all over. No matter which direction I looked, I felt as if someone was staring holes in my back.

"Where is a private place to see if the case will open?" Eddie asked as soon as the key had been returned, darting wild glances up and down the concourse. "What are those blue doors that don't say anything on them? Could we go into one of those rooms?"

"I think they're private lounges, something

like that," Charlie said. "I'm pretty sure they're locked, but we could try a few of them."

It didn't take long to find out that we couldn't get into one of those places without a key, or pushing a button to get someone to open the door for us. I was more and more anxious to get that briefcase out of sight. "How about down at the end, in that boarding area where there isn't anybody right now?" I'd begun to wish we hadn't disguised ourselves, because while we looked different from the kids who'd arrived on Flight 211, we sure hadn't made ourselves invisible.

"Okay," Charlie accepted, and we hurried in that direction.

According to the sign, there wouldn't be a flight leaving from this gate for an hour and a half, Flight 107 for Albuquerque. We sank into chairs, Charlie in the middle with the case on his lap.

"It's locked," he said.

"Naturally," Eddie said. "Are we going to try to pick the lock?"

"Maybe," I said uneasily, "we should take it to the security police."

Charlie gave me an exaggeratedly charming smile. "Sure, Gracie. And tell them what? We just found it? They wouldn't even investigate, see what's in it. They'd leave it at the lost and found department, if they have such a thing, until someone shows up and describes it well enough so they'll take his word for it that it belongs to him. It has initials on it—see, L.J.S. So all that would happen would be that L.J.S. produces identification with those initials and says it's his, and they give it to him. After what we've been through, we're not handing it to the cops and never finding out what this is all about."

We'd been so engrossed in ourselves we'd forgotten to be on guard, and when the voice spoke behind me I almost collapsed in a puddle on the floor.

# Chapter Fifteen

"I think it's time we had a talk," the voice said, and I turned slowly to look up into the face of the man in the gray suit.

I felt as if everything in me had suddenly dried up, as if my heart had stopped beating and I couldn't get my breath.

Charlie looked startled and scared, too, but at least he could still speak. "Who're you?" he asked.

I looked around to see if it was worthwhile to scream for help, but we'd picked this area because there weren't any people in it right now, and there still weren't. Oh, we could see a few travelers off in the distance, but there was no one close to us, and certainly none of the security officers I'd hoped for.

Whatever this man intended to do, nobody

was likely to stop him. I gulped audibly.

The stranger who had accosted us reached inside his jacket, and I felt myself turning to mush. Was he going to shoot us, right here?

It wasn't a gun he produced, though. Instead it looked like a black leather wallet. Only when he opened it up it wasn't money inside. There was a silver-colored badge, very official looking, and an I.D. card with his picture on it. I was too stunned to read it all, but he told us the important part.

"Agent James Santori, Federal Bureau of Investigation."

Eddie exhaled a tremulous breath. "You mean you're not going to shoot us?"

For a moment the man's face was so serious I thought Eddie might be wrong about that, and then Agent Santori's mouth twitched a little. "Not right this minute," he said. "But I want to talk to you."

Charlie's fingers tightened on the handle of the briefcase we'd appropriated from the locker. He cleared his throat. "What about?" he asked, as if he had no idea.

"About a couple of men you may remember.

One of them traveled with you on the plane down from Seattle. The other one came in shortly behind you in Portland, on a charter flight, and came on from there on your continuing flight."

We looked at each other and nodded. I had started to breathe again. I wasn't as scared of an F.B.I. agent as I was of The Enemy who had attacked Mrs. Basker, but I wasn't sure what they did to you if you'd taken a briefcase that didn't belong to you out of a locker. Had he watched us empty the locker? Did he realize it wasn't our case? Had he heard what Charlie said just before he approached us?

"Sure," Charlie said finally. "Mr. Upton and the guy in the Hawaiian shirt."

"Those are the ones," Agent Santori agreed. "What do you know about them?"

I would have just told him, but Charlie was stubborn. He said later he figured the guy would take the briefcase and we'd never know what it was about unless he resisted at least a little.

"What's going on? Why are you investigating them?"

Eddie was braver than I was, too. "Are they drug dealers or something like that?" he wanted to know.

The F.B.I. man ignored him. He seemed to sense that Charlie was the leader and spoke directly to him. "You're aware that these men have been following you, and that they're dangerous." He hesitated. "Very dangerous."

"Sure," Charlie admitted.

"So what do you know about them? What called your attention to them in the first place?"

I opened my mouth to reply, but Agent Santori wasn't looking at me, and then Charlie said the most outrageous thing. My mouth was still open, only now it was sagging at Charlie's nerve.

"What's in it for us?" Charlie asked.

For a minute I thought the F.B.I. agent was going to put handcuffs on him and search him. He didn't say anything and Charlie pushed harder.

"If we tell you everything and you don't tell us anything, it's not a very fair trade," Charlie said. "What kind of case are we mixed up in?"

Agent Santori's face was as scary as when

I'd first noticed him watching us. "Blackmail is a criminal offense, you know."

"I'm not asking for money," Charlie told him brazenly, "just information. Is it a drug case? Or what?"

The man's voice went very soft. "Are you saying you won't cooperate by answering questions?"

"No, sir. But it's not fair not to tell us anything, in exchange for what *we* know. It's not a matter of national security, I'm pretty sure of that. They're just crooks, right? Tell us what's going on, and we'll be happy to tell you what we've found out, right, gang?"

Even while he had me worried that he'd get us all locked up, I had to confess to a certain admiration for his effrontery. (That was one of those words I learned when Grandma was doing her puzzles.) I'd never have dared talk to him that way, and I didn't think Eddie would have, either. My dad once referred to Charlie as "all brass and a mile wide," and I finally saw what he meant.

Eddie did find the courage to back Charlie up, though. "Sure. We'll tell what we've found out."

Between the two of them they made it sound like we'd found out a lot, and I supposed maybe we had if the contents of the briefcase were as valuable—or as incriminating—as we guessed.

Agent Santori was regarding Charlie as if he were some loathsome variety of worm. "You kids traveling alone? No chaperones?"

"No. I'm thirteen. We don't need a baby-sitter," Charlie said.

"Then you're mature enough to know that the best thing to do when a federal agent asks questions is to answer them."

"Sure. I told you we'll cooperate fully. So what's the big deal about a trade of information? Just tell us what kind of a case it is. Not the names of the criminals, necessarily, but what the case is about. Besides the fact that they hit old Mrs. Basker over the head and put her in the hospital to get her bag, what's going on?"

The state I was in, it was a miracle I could notice anything except that I was in a cold sweat of nervousness. But I was pretty sure that Charlie had just given him *one* bit of information he hadn't had before. He didn't know about Mrs. Basker.

His next words proved it. "When did they do this? Hit this old lady?"

"In Portland Airport, a few hours ago," Eddie said, before Charlie barked, "We're going to trade information, remember?"

The F.B.I. agent considered this for long seconds. In the silence I heard a jet taking off, far in the distance.

"All right," Agent Santori said finally, not sounding the least bit friendly. "I'll give you a couple of basic facts, and then you'll answer my questions. Either here, and in full, or in my office at the Federal Building. You got that straight?"

Charlie nodded, and I let out a little of the breath I'd been holding.

"Okay. You've stumbled into a case involving large sums of money, taken in on stolen merchandise that has been sold across state lines and international borders, which makes the crime fall under the jurisdiction of the Federal Bureau of Investigation. This illegally earned money is being moved around the country by couriers so that it can be put back into circulation through legitimate businesses—"

"Money laundering!" Charlie exclaimed. "Isn't that what they call it?"

"Correct. There is considerable money involved, and the men who are doing it have a lot at stake. They are very dangerous. Nobody for a bunch of kids to get mixed up with, because they could easily get hurt." He was back to his former point. "And that is why you are now going to sit down and tell me exactly how you got involved with these people and what you've learned about them."

"Sure," Charlie said. His eyes were glowing. I thought he was probably already wondering if he'd get his picture in the paper.

At that moment the voice on the P.A. system caught our attention: "Will Charlie Portwood come to the nearest white courtesy telephone, please? Charlie Portwood?"

"It's for us! It's Aunt Molly, she's finally here!" I cried in relief. "We have to go find one of those white phones right away!" I no longer cared about the contents of the briefcase or The Enemy. I wanted to turn the whole mess over to Aunt Molly and let her deal with it, including the F.B.I. agent.

"Just a minute," Agent Santori began, but Charlie spoke urgently. "We'll talk to you in a minute, sir, but right now we have to answer the page. Our aunt's expecting us, and she won't know where we are. She'll be worried. Besides," Charlie added, "we should have an adult present when we answer questions anyway, shouldn't we?"

Agent Santori gave him the kind of look my dad gave me when I mentioned wanting to have my hair dyed red. "You want your lawyer present, too?"

Charlie grinned. I suppose that he, too, felt better knowing rescue was at hand in the form of Aunt Molly. "It wouldn't hurt," he agreed.

"Come on," I urged. "We've got to answer the page."

Agent Santori nodded sardonically. "All right. Go ahead. As soon as your aunt joins you, we'll talk." He made it sound like a threat.

He came along behind us as we hurried to find one of the white phones, but he didn't make any effort to keep up. I was eager to talk to Aunt Molly, but it was Charlie who got there first.

"Hi, Aunt Molly. Yeah, we got here all right. Is your friend okay? Good. Uh, yeah, we're near Gate . . ."

He turned around to see what the nearest gate number was, and froze.

I turned slowly, too, and saw Eddie's face change before my own must have.

Mr. Upton was there, and the guy in the Hawaiian shirt, but not the F.B.I. agent. I glanced around wildly for Agent Santori, who was nowhere in sight even though he'd only been a few yards behind us.

Mr. Upton spoke very softly. "Hang up the phone, kid."

The gun he was pointing at Charlie's belt buckle was quite enough to assure our cooperation.

And without a word, before he could tell Aunt Molly where we were, Charlie replaced the receiver.

# Chapter Sixteen

This was real, I thought numbly. My dad's worst fears—and my own—had come true.

Two men, one of them with a gun, were making us walk with them along one of the broad corridors. The one in the Hawaiian shirt had taken possession of the briefcase. Both of them were grim-faced, and after Mr. Upton said, "Just come along with us and don't make any ruckus," nobody said a word.

As Charlie said later, at least he could have added, "and nobody will get hurt." He didn't even give us that much assurance that things would eventually work out all right.

I saw the old lady with the dirty coat and her belongings in a couple of paper shopping bags; she grinned at us as if she remembered us, but she didn't seem to see anything unusual in the way we were being hurried along by the two men.

We passed a security guard, who paid no attention, and dozens of other people, all bent on getting to their flight, or meeting someone else's. No one seemed to notice what must have been three very scared young faces.

What had happened to Agent Santori? He knew what these men looked like, he'd told us they were dangerous, yet now that we were really in trouble he'd disappeared, though he had been right behind us only a few minutes ago.

What if he wasn't really an F.B.I. agent? His badge and I.D. had looked genuine, but I supposed anything could be faked. What if he was in cahoots with The Enemy, as I'd believed in the beginning? Or had they somehow managed to put him out of action—hit him over the head the way they'd done with Mrs. Basker— or even killed him?

Aunt Molly had to be somewhere in the terminal, I thought in rising panic. Had she heard Mr. Upton's low command to hang up the phone? Or only the click when the receiver was replaced? Would she think Charlie had hung up accidentally, or would she know we were in danger?

I'd expected that when Aunt Molly showed up we'd be okay. She was an adult. She'd know what to do. But she didn't know where we were, and this airline terminal was as big as some small towns.

Even if she reported to the security police, where would they start to look for us? Would they find us in time?

I glanced at Charlie, who was walking briskly with Mr. Upton right behind him. He sensed that I had turned my head, and opened his mouth to say something, but Mr. Upton said in a tone that permitted no back talk, "Keep still."

The men were moving as if they had a definite destination in mind. What if they took us away from the airport? How would Aunt Molly or the cops find us then? If I'd ever thought Agent Santori was bluffing when he told us these men were very dangerous, I didn't think so now.

I remembered how huge San Francisco had looked from the air when our plane banked to approach the airport. Thousands of people, I thought, my mouth so dry I couldn't even swallow. Thousands of places where they could hide three kids. Three bodies.

It's quite terrifying to think of yourself and your cousins as *bodies*.

Max had always wanted to be an only child. Maybe now he was going to get his wish.

"Go left here," Mr. Upton said, and we turned into one of the side corridors. For a moment I felt a leap of hope, because some distance ahead I could see one of the security gates you have to go through so they can X-ray your baggage to see if you're carrying weapons. But of course we weren't going that far.

"Hold it," Hawaiian shirt said, and we stopped in front of one of those locked blue doors. Mr. Upton had a key, which he used, and the door swung inward. He nudged Charlie forward, ahead of him, and then Eddie and me.

We were in a rather large room with couches and chairs covered with sheets of plastic. Two of the walls had been painted pale blue. The carpet had been torn up and a padding had been partially put back down, with several rolls of it stacked close to one of the newly painted walls.

I heard the door click shut behind us and knew without checking that it had automatically locked. I was sure it would keep other people out, unless they had keys; would it also keep us in? Or could the door be opened from the inside? I wished the blood wasn't pounding so hard in my ears; it was difficult to hear, or even to think.

Not that anyone was saying anything so far. Hawaiian shirt swung the briefcase onto one of the plastic-covered tables; Mr. Upton produced a key to it and opened it up.

I don't think they intended us to know what was in it. Eddie and I couldn't see, from where we were standing, but Charlie could. I saw his eyes practically bug out; he swallowed and averted his eyes. I thought he was trying to send us a message and I mouthed, "Drugs?"

His head moved ever so slightly from side to side.

"Money?" Eddie whispered.

That was a mistake, and Eddie knew it as soon as we did.

Both men turned, and their faces were menacing. Mr. Upton slammed the briefcase shut, but he'd stepped to one side and the lid didn't come down before I'd glimpsed the contents of the case.

It was money. More money than I'd ever seen in my life, all in neat packets. Laundering the cash they'd gotten from some kind of illegal business, Agent Santori had said, meaning they would make the cash seem legitimately earned by processing it through a legal business.

They knew we had seen it. Hawaiian shirt grimaced. "You kids should have minded your own business."

There didn't seem to be any sensible response to that, so we just stood there. It dawned on me that this wasn't anywhere near as much fun as watching the same kind of situation on TV.

"What are we going to do with 'em?" Hawaiian shirt asked.

"We better call the boss," Mr. Upton said after a moment's hesitation.

"He doesn't like it very much when somebody screws up," Hawaiian shirt reminded him.

Mr. Upton gave him a savage look. "Well, who screwed up, buddy? You're the one who left the newspaper where the kid could pick it up. And who let her keep it long enough to erase part of the message?"

"I wasn't supposed to have to leave Seattle," Hawaiian shirt said, getting angry, too. "You should have retrieved the paper before the kid got off the plane!"

Mr. Upton's lips drew back in a snarl. "I thought the old woman had it! You stay here with the kids while I go find a phone. I don't want to use the one in here. In fact I don't even know if it's still working. We can consider ourselves lucky that they're redecorating the room right now so we have a place to be undisturbed. The workmen won't be back before Monday morning."

He made it sound as if *we* would still be here Monday morning. Maybe, I thought, fighting dizziness, just our bodies lying here for the workmen to find when they came to finish their job. I could tell by Eddie's face that he was thinking the same thing.

"Leave me the gun," Hawaiian shirt said.

Mr. Upton gave him a scornful sneer, but he handed it over. "I should think even you could handle three little kids," he said. I didn't think they liked working together very well. From Charlie's face I figured he was calculating how that might be to our advantage.

I wasn't too petrified to notice one thing. When Mr. Upton left the room, he didn't use the key to open the door. It wasn't locked from the inside, only from the outside.

I looked at Charlie and Eddie and saw they'd noticed it, too. Charlie took a few steps, and though he didn't move toward our captor, but away from him, it made Hawaiian shirt uneasy.

"Stay where you are, kid," he said.

Charlie shrugged, as if it didn't matter. I thought I saw what he was maneuvering toward, though. In the corner there were some cleaning tools, like brooms and a long-handled squeegee to clean windows and a paint roller that had a long handle, too, for doing ceilings and upper walls.

We'd used broom handles, with no brooms left on them, for the villain's and the prince's swords in our play. My heart had already been pounding; now it was like thunder. It made so much noise in my ears I was afraid if Charlie whispered anything I wouldn't hear it.

Charlie went up and down a little on the balls of his feet, his legs spread apart for balance. He looked absurd in the plaid shorts and the San Francisco Giants shirt with the orange baseball cap. "How you doing, princess?" he asked me.

The man with the gun jerked it toward Charlie. "Shut up," he said.

The play. How well did I still remember the play? We'd done it two whole years ago. But Charlie was feeding me a line from it, and beside me I was aware of Eddie tensing to spring. I was afraid my own muscles were paralyzed. What if we made a move and the man fired?

"Don't you kids try anything cute," Hawaiian shirt said, and he sounded nasty. "This room's practically soundproof—you notice you can't hardly hear the jets taking off?—and I won't hesitate to shoot all three of you if I have to."

"That's what you're planning to do eventually anyhow, isn't it?" Charlie asked. There was a gleam in his eyes much like he'd had the time he proposed we all jump off the bridge into the Pilchuck River, when Dad came along and stopped us and told us we'd have broken our necks because the water was too shallow.

No, Charlie, no! I was saying silently, but the rest of me—except for my mind—got ready for whatever was coming.

"Don't be stupid, kid. The boss may tell us to let you go."

And he may not, I thought, wanting to scream from the tension. Because we can describe you and your cronies, and we know you've got a whole briefcase full of money, and you knocked Mrs. Basker over the head, and we know you've got a key to get into this room. Probably not very many people have keys. If we talk to anybody, they'll catch you sooner or later. And put you in prison for a long, long time. And you know that.

Charlie was looking at me, and I knew what he was waiting for. He didn't dare say that final line aloud, not with that gun pointing at him, but he was thinking it right at me, and I understood.

In the play I only partly remembered, the villain had sworn to keep me captive forever, and I'd screamed for the prince to come to my rescue.

I opened my mouth and shrieked.

"Help! Help, save me!"

Hawaiian shirt was as nervous as we were, I guess. He didn't shoot, but he was startled enough to lose his cool. He jerked toward me so the gun was wavering between me and Charlie.

We all moved at once, and in different directions.

Charlie grabbed the squeegee and swung it, connecting with Hawaiian shirt's mouth. Eddie had the broom and slammed it into the side of the man's head. I grabbed the only thing I could reach that was loose and not covered by plastic, which was a long decorative ceiling light fixture that had been taken down for the painting. It was heavier than I expected, which slowed me down, but it made a satisfying *crash* when I brought it down on the hand holding the gun.

It got a little confusing for a minute or so after that.

The gun skidded across the floor and Charlie kicked it. Eddie yelled "Bonzai!" and swung the broom again. Charlie came back with the squeegee from the other side, and they caught our enemy's ears from both sides in a sort of sandwich effect.

Just then the door began to swing inward. I saw it moving and closed my eyes. If Mr. Upton had orders from the boss to eliminate us, it was all over. They'd shoot us here in this practically soundproof room. We would be dead, and my little brother, Max, would get my room and my tape player and my—

But the voice that spoke wasn't Mr. Upton's. It belonged to Agent Santori. My eyes popped open.

He didn't look as if he'd been shot or hit over the head. And he wasn't alone. There were two other men with him. The only one who had drawn his gun was the young guy Charlie had declared innocent and harmless, the one in the patched jeans and colorless sweatshirt.

We all froze as if we were playing that old game Statues. The man who had held us captive until a minute ago was the stillest one of all.

Everyone but The Enemy let out the breath they'd been holding.

Eddie and Charlie put down their weapons. Hawaiian shirt was swearing and wiping at his bloody nose.

"Where were you?" Charlie demanded of the F.B.I. agent. "I thought you'd never get here in time!"

"I was afraid they'd killed you," I admitted, my voice wavering. "And then they were going to kill us!"

Agent Santori gave me a small, tight smile. "Sorry I had to let you get so scared before I showed up, but we needed as much incriminating evidence as possible. We may be able to pin a kidnapping charge on them now, too. That's an offense that should add a few years to your sentence, Donovan," he said to the man who was glaring at us over a bloody handkerchief. "Get him out of here," he told the young man who looked like a leftover hippie.

"There's another one, a guy who calls

himself Mr. Upton," Charlie said as the other two agents led our captor away. "He went to call his boss, to see what to do with us—"

"I think they were going to shoot us," Eddie added eagerly. He was still pale, but he was grinning.

We followed the men out into the corridor, and stopped. Because there were more agents here—and they had Mr. Upton spread-eagled against a wall, searching him. He was swearing, too.

One of the men swatted him on the shoulder. "Ah, ah, don't use that kind of language in front of juveniles, Morales."

"His name's Morales?" Eddie asked. "Not Upton?"

"That's one of his names," Agent Santori said dryly. "Come on, get them out of here, fellas. I have some questions to ask you kids, though. Let's go up to the security offices, where we won't have an audience."

I finally found my tongue. "Our aunt's looking for us—Molly Portwood, she had us paged, only when Charlie got on the phone Mr. Upton—Morales—made him hang up."

"We'll find your aunt as soon as we've talked," Agent Santori informed us.

Actually, we found her before he asked us any questions. She was just coming out of the security police office, looking concerned until she saw us.

"Oh, there you are! I had you paged again after we were cut off, but you didn't call back." She stopped and looked at us. "Good grief, I left you here alone too long, didn't I? What will your folks think when you go home with those outfits? Well, I'm sorry it took me so long, but we got delayed in traffic as well as at the emergency room. I didn't worry about you, I knew how self-sufficient Charlie is—"

About that time it dawned on her that the tall, good-looking man with us was *with* us.

"Is . . . is something wrong here?"

I've said before that Aunt Molly is pretty. She has dark brown hair and dark eyes, and she was wearing one of those outfits that Aunt Joan thinks are "too extreme"—this one was butter yellow and had a swirly pleated skirt and only narrow straps over her shoulders—and I could tell Agent Santori thought she was pretty, too.

He flashed his I.D. again and she let her mouth fall open. Even that way, she was pretty.

"Miss . . . Portwood, is it? And these youngsters are your niece and nephews?"

"Yes, that's right. What's going on? Has something happened?"

"You might say that," Charlie told her cheerfully. I was breathing normally again, too, although I felt sort of shaky.

"I need to ask them some questions," Agent Santori said. "It'll take a little while."

"Now? You mean I can't take them home and feed them? Look, they aren't in trouble, are they?" Aunt Molly demanded. "I mean, you're not *arresting* them, are you?"

"No, no. But we do need to learn some particulars of the case we've just wound up. Perhaps—" He hesitated. "Well, of course it is getting late, and they're probably hungry. Tell you what, Miss Portwood—it is *miss,* isn't it? Why don't I take your address and I'll give you a couple of hours to get them fed, and then I'll ask my questions at your place. More comfortable than headquarters, anyway."

Aunt Molly considered, looking up at him

through sweeping dark lashes that Aunt Joan swears are artificial, and Mom says are real except for the mascara. "Well, I only intend to feed them pizza. We could always pick up enough for one more, if you'd like to join us, Agent Santori. That way I wouldn't have to give you directions to my place; you could just follow us."

He didn't hesitate very long. "That sounds like a great idea. I'll pick up the pizza. Pepperoni or Canadian bacon? Or anchovies?"

The way he said it, nobody would have dared asked for anchovies. Aunt Molly was the only one who liked them, anyway, and she didn't say a word when the rest of us voted for pepperoni.

In the car, on the way to Aunt Molly's new house, I poked Charlie in the ribs with an elbow and leaned toward him to whisper. "I think she likes Agent Santori."

He never even heard me. "I hope he's going to explain it all. The case, I mean. I'll bet we guessed right about just about everything, but I'd like to hear the details. It wasn't drugs, so what was it they were stealing and selling across state lines and even out of the country? It had to be something worth a lot to make up a whole briefcase full of money. What I saw was in hundred-dollar bills."

I doubted if real agents explained things to civilians the way they do on TV, but I didn't say so. I wanted to know the details, too.

I wondered if there was any way to keep my dad from hearing everything that had happened to us, and sighed.

He wasn't going to be happy about it, even if it had turned out okay. Maybe we'd be lucky and they wouldn't mention us when the story came on television.

# Chapter Seventeen

Aunt Molly's new house was on the top of a hill—San Francisco has lots of hills—and when it got dark we could see the lights coming on all over the city below. The bridges looked like sparkling diamonds across the black water of the bay.

By that time, we'd finished our second supper—nobody mentioned how much we'd eaten at the airport—and Aunt Molly had called each set of parents to warn them that we might be mentioned on the news, but that there was nothing to worry about.

I was glad she talked to my dad, not me. I didn't want to know what he thought until he'd had a chance to calm down. I heard her say, "It wasn't anything the kids did wrong, Don. They saw a crime committed, and the authorities are asking them some questions, that's all. No, they don't need a lawyer present, they aren't accused of anything, nor suspects in the case. In fact, they helped solve it. They'll tell you about it later, okay?"

At least he didn't demand to speak to me personally. I was grateful for that.

What I wanted, though, was for Agent Santori to start explaining things. We were sitting around this big living room looking out at the lights, mostly on cushions on the floor because she didn't have much furniture yet except for a blue couch from her old apartment; she sat on one end of that, and Agent Santori—who was generally called Jim, we'd found out—on the other end.

He leaned forward and took the last piece of pizza, then got out a small notebook and started to ask questions, occasionally writing something down. We answered truthfully, sneaking a glance at Aunt Molly once in a while when we thought she might not approve of what we'd done.

She rolled her eyes a lot, and when we told about finding Mrs. Basker unconscious she made a squeaking sound the way I do when I can't come up with the right words. When he finally closed the notebook and stuck it into an inside pocket, though, she had her own questions.

"Okay, now what was it all about? Where did the money come from? Who does it belong to?"

Eddie sat cross-legged on a big yellow pillow. "Was it a drug deal? A million dollars?"

"I'm afraid I can't tell you any more than I already have," Agent Santori said, and we all groaned, including Aunt Molly.

"That's hardly fair," she said, sounding like Charlie. "You could at least give us an idea of what they got mixed up in. You said yourself they helped you turn up the evidence you need to prosecute what must be an important case. The F.B.I. doesn't get involved in minor cases, does it?"

He grinned, and he didn't look scary now, I thought. Maybe it was the pizza sauce on his chin. Aunt Molly handed him a napkin and he wiped his mouth.

"The F.B.I. gets involved in all kinds of cases," he said, "and we aren't allowed to talk about any of them. What the kids have told me has been very valuable, and it's quite possible they'll be called upon either to testify or to give depositions. That means giving a statement to a court official and swearing that it's true."

"We know that," Charlie said witheringly. I could see he was as disappointed as I was that we weren't going to hear the juicy details. After all, we'd come close to getting killed trying to get them. "I hope they're going to call us as witnesses. Do you get paid for being a witness?"

Aunt Molly rolled her eyes again, but Agent Santori replied seriously. "No, but if they should decide to have you testify in person they'd pay your expenses to come back to San Francisco to do it."

"Aren't we even going to be able to find out how Mrs. Basker is?" I demanded.

He drained his Pepsi can and stood up. "If you don't mind my using the phone, I'm sure I can find out about that for you."

"Sure," Aunt Molly said, and directed him to the telephone in the kitchen.

When he came back, he said, "Mrs. Basker

is staying in the hospital overnight for observation, and she'll probably finish her flight home tomorrow. She's awake and remembers very clearly the man who threatened her and hit her over the head. One of our agents is there with her now, and she'll be testifying, too, no doubt. Tell you what. You'll read about most of this in the papers over the next week or so. Before you go back to Seattle, if your aunt doesn't mind, I'll come over again some evening and tell you anything additional that I'm allowed to reveal. How will that be? You've guessed most of it anyhow."

It wasn't very satisfying, but it was the best he'd agree to. Charlie was still grumbling when the three of us went to bed, leaving Agent Santori and Aunt Molly still talking.

I kind of wished I had a girl cousin to stay with me in the empty room where I'd spread a sleeping bag. Even Cheryl would have been better than no company that first night; I suspected I might have nightmares after what we'd been through that day.

After I got into my pajamas, I went out to get a drink and heard Aunt Molly and Agent

Santori laughing. I stopped in the darkness of the hallway and listened.

"You wouldn't believe the audacity of that kid," he told her, and I knew he was talking about Charlie. "Absolutely demanded to know about the case before he'd tell me what he knew. And he stood right there holding that case that probably had a million dollars in it and let me think it was his own! Those kids had every intention of opening it up and seeing what was in it before they told me what they had."

He laughed, and so did Aunt Molly "That's our Charlie," she affirmed.

Why is it that grown-ups will bawl you out like crazy for doing something, and then laugh when they tell another grown-up about it? I remember, my mom did that when she told Dad that Max had cornered a skunk in the toolshed. Come to think of it, I don't believe *Dad* was too amused. Grown-ups are sort of hard to figure out sometimes. Of course it was *his* tools in the shed, not Mom's.

I got my drink and went on to bed, and to my complete surprise I didn't have bad dreams after all.

For the next three days we grabbed the morning paper before we set out for Golden Gate Park or Fisherman's Wharf and for riding on the cable cars and taking a cruise around San Francisco Bay. We divided it into sections to look for the story, but it was never there.

And then on the day we'd been at the beach and gotten half-sick on hot dogs and potato chips, and nobody wanted any supper, Eddie turned on the TV and gave a cry of triumph. "Hey, listen to this! This has got to be it, doesn't it?"

And there it was, the feature story on the six o'clock news.

A man named Bernard Berry, who owned automobile dealerships all up and down the West Coast, had been indicted, and a number of his employees with him. It sounded as if Mr. Berry had gotten rich selling new and used cars, but he wasn't satisfied with that. So he went into another business on the side: selling stolen cars. Some of them were shipped out of the country, into Mexico and Canada. Others were taken across state lines for sale in other parts of the United States. And his illegal profits were then moved in to be "laundered" through his genuine businesses by couriers like Mr. Upton and Hawaiian shirt, whose name turned out to be Claude Donovan.

Mr. Berry belonged to the club that used the room where we'd been held captive. He provided his employees with keys for just such emergencies as we had caused by interfering in their delivery of one shipment of illegal cash to a legitimate car agency in Seattle.

Eddie sounded crushed when the announcer went on to a story about the latest jumper off the Golden Gate Bridge. "They never even mentioned *us!*"

"You'd think it would make a better story to say that three kids helped the F.B.I. capture them," Charlie groaned. "They ought to give us a little credit! After all, we'd taken old Hawaiian-shirt-Donovan off guard and knocked the gun out of his hand before the F.B.I. even got there!"

Aunt Molly had kicked off her shoes and was wiggling her toes. "They've only just been indicted. It'll be months, probably, before they come to trial. Maybe then they'll mention you kids when the full story comes out."

Eddie had his forehead all wrinkled up. "They didn't explain everything," he said. "Like, who put the money in the locker in San Francisco?"

"Somebody who worked for Mr. Berry," Charlie said immediately. "I bet he had to stash it there in an emergency, see, like he was taking it out of the Bay Area"—that's what all the local people call the cities around San Francisco and Oakland on the other side of the bay—"and he knew the F.B.I. agents were on his tail—"

Charlie spun a wonderful yarn, Aunt Molly said, but we'd probably never learn the whole truth. Actually, we did find out most of it, and as usual Charlie wasn't far from wrong. The real story was so complicated and so almost silly, it made me wonder why anyone would want to be a criminal.

One of Mr. Berry's couriers, named Lenny Kalt, was taking the money his boss had earned selling stolen cars in a second-hand briefcase—the initials didn't mean a thing, which Eddie thought was very disappointing, since they'd ought to have been a clue—up north to Seattle to deliver to Claude Donovan, or Hawaiian shirt, as we continued to think of him. Only two things happened.

Lenny saw someone watching him—the guy we'd thought was a leftover hippie—and it made him nervous. Then he got sick, and he was in such pain (turned out he had a ruptured appendix and had to be taken to the hospital and operated on, which was where they arrested him), he knew he couldn't carry out his assignment.

He tried to call one of Mr. Berry's other employees to have him come to the airport and take his place, carrying the money to Seattle. But he couldn't get anyone on the phone, and Lenny knew he had to do something right away. I guess he was so sick he could hardly think straight, but he did the best he could.

He put the money in a locker, and because he was afraid that if he got caught the police would figure out what it was for and find all that cash, he didn't dare keep the key on him. So he did the only thing he could think of before he collapsed and the security people at the airport called for an ambulance.

He bought some Scotch tape and taped the key under the counter in a phone booth near the lockers, and wrote down the phone number there on a postcard he got in the gift shop where he got the tape.

What he should have done then, Charlie thought, was send the postcard to Mr. Berry or someone else in San Francisco who worked for him. It turned out, though, that Mr. Berry was a very hard man to work for. He didn't like people who made mistakes, even a mistake like having an appendix rupture. Lenny was afraid he'd lose his job, or even worse. Charlie, of course, was sure Lenny would have wound up on the bottom of San Francisco Bay tied to a chunk of cement.

"People who are really sick," Aunt Molly said, "don't always come up with the best ideas. Besides, what Lenny did probably would have worked fine—and his boss would never have known the difference—if Gracie hadn't picked up that newspaper at Sea-Tac before the man it was intended for got to it."

So I guess in a way I *did* help catch the

guilty parties. Because Lenny was trying to keep from losing his job—or worse—he sent the postcard to Donovan-Hawaiian shirt, trusting him to figure out that it was a locker number and a phone number at San Francisco Airport, where it was mailed.

Donovan figured it out, all right, but he didn't get it for a couple of days after the money was supposed to have been delivered to him. Before the postcard showed up, Donovan was frantic. It was a lot of money, and he was afraid Mr. Berry would hold him responsible, and then *he* might have wound up at the bottom of Puget Sound.

Anyway, when the postcard came, he realized what it meant. Only he didn't want to go to the San Francisco Airport and be the one to retrieve the money. He was afraid it might be dangerous. If the police had spotted Lenny before he was taken to the hospital, they might have staked out the locker and phone booth. Mr. Donovan didn't want to be the one arrested if that turned out to be the case and whoever collected the money was caught with it. So he got Mr. Upton to do it.

To make sure it was all kept secret, he made up the code in the paper, folded it, and left it on a particular seat in the waiting room where our flight was going to take off.

Charlie said they did a lot of what he called "cloak and dagger stuff," meaning the conspirators didn't want to be seen together in case they were being watched by the authorities. Mr. Donovan called Mr. Upton and told him where to pick up the newspaper.

When Mr. Donovan realized *I* had picked up the paper moments before Mr. Upton should have done it, he was furious. He had to risk a personal meeting with Mr. Upton, and told him to hurry up and get a ticket on Flight 211 and get it back. Mr. Upton was supposed to go on another flight. He knew I'd given the paper to Mrs. Basker, but then she gave me back the crossword puzzle with the code message on it, and everything was pretty confused.

When they realized Mrs. Basker didn't have what they wanted, they figured out that *I* must, so they came after us. (Once Donovan wrote the message in the paper, he destroyed the card, so he didn't remember the telephone and locker numbers, either.) But that was in Portland, and after. We sure hated to think what would have happened if the F.B.I. hadn't been lurking around keeping an eye on the whole situation.

The Portland business happened because Mr. Donovan decided he didn't totally trust Mr. Upton, and that maybe he'd better be there, watching him pick up the money, but at a safe enough distance so he wouldn't be caught if Upton was arrested. But by then our flight was gone. So Mr. Donovan decided to slow down our flight enough that a chartered plane would catch up with us. He called the airport and reported a bomb on board our plane. He knew that would make them land as soon as they could, and the only airport big enough was Portland. So he came to Portland.

We were delayed there of course, while the crew searched for the reported bomb, and we saw Donovan shortly after his arrival. Mr. Upton was mad because it was clear Donovan didn't trust him, and I guess they argued about what to do next. What they did do, we knew. But whose idea it all was, we weren't sure. We only knew they were sure angry at each other after they were arrested. Each one blamed the other one for getting caught.

As I said, though, we didn't know all this while we were watching the TV newscast. All we could do was guess.

"You think the newspapers will interview us?" Charlie asked, brightening. "Maybe we'll be on national TV!"

"You better hope you're not," Aunt Molly said dryly, "or your folks will never let you come down here again."

"Why not?" I asked. "What could go wrong just flying from Seattle to San Francisco?"

We all cracked up, laughing.

Actually, the next time we went to San Francisco was six months later, and our whole families went, too, for Aunt Molly's wedding. Now we call Agent Santori Uncle Jim, but he still doesn't tell us anything about his cases.

As Charlie says, it's too bad we didn't get to fly by ourselves again. Who knows what might have happened?